DEADLY BETRAYAL, SCVC TASKFORCE ROMANTIC SUSPENSE SERIES, BOOK 12

MISTY EVANS

Deadly Betrayal, SCVC Taskforce Romantic Suspense Series, Book 12

Misty Evans

ISBN: 978-1-948686-36-5

Cover Art by Fanderclai Design

Formatting by Beach Path Publishing, LLC

Editing by Elizabeth Neal, Patricia Essex

Please Note

ONE

Josie stood outside *Bad Medicine*, the sports bar her brother, Bruno, frequented. She stared at the turquoise blue door, listening to the muffled jukebox music floating out, and had the fleeting thought she'd rather be flying over Afghanistan again, rather than going in to find him.

The parking lot was filled with an assortment of trucks, motorcycles, and four-wheel drive SUVs. From the license plates and various stickers decorating them, the place was filled with military veterans. All branches were represented, but she suspected the Navy and Marines claimed the majority.

Being former Army, she wasn't excited to dive in to that crowd. Bruno had mentioned there was constant teasing and bickering between the branches. No surprise there. Each believed wholeheartedly that theirs was the most elite, hands-down, badass group around.

Problem was, she was on her last five dollars, two prescription pain meds left, her disability check – make that the past three – still hadn't shown up, and the final blow to her disastrous life had come only hours ago when she discovered she'd been betrayed. The one shining dream she'd held since she'd returned to the states from her final tour had fizzled to a dark, tangled, sticky mass of goo inside her chest.

Bruno was a last resort, although he was always more than willing to lend a hand. She hated depending on others, asking for help, but life was pushing her beyond the limits of what she could handle.

"*You ain't a Marine,*" she could hear her brother tease.

No, but she was still hard as nails.

Unfortunately, she'd recently realized even nails got bent in the wrong direction at times.

The sound of a truck door slamming echoed behind her. She probably looked like an idiot, standing here debating whether or not to go in.

What did she care what a stranger thought, though? No one here knew her, and she didn't have the energy to care what people assumed about her. She'd served her country, arrived stateside injured, and now she was getting screwed. Her determination and independence had taken a whopping hit the past few months since moving to San Diego, and she knew she truly had nowhere else to turn.

Sensing someone strolling up behind her, she moved to the left. At least, she attempted to. Her bum leg refused, and she had to drag it sideways in order to get out of the way.

She'd left her cane in her car, too much of her pride left. She refused to walk in there looking disabled, especially when she knew many of the men and women inside had lost far more than she had. Her disability was nothing to be ashamed of, and yet, she hadn't fully accepted her limitations. Her stubbornness kept her from using the cane most of the time, no matter how bad the pain got.

The sound of boots thudded on the rickety wooden risers.

A man's voice asked, "You going in, buttercup?"

Buttercup? From the corner of her eye, she shot him a glare. Tall, broad, full of himself. Not hard to detect that from the way he grinned and pretended to be a gentleman, waving a hand at the door like a butler and waiting for her to go first.

"Haven't made up my mind. Go ahead, *rosebud.*"

"Ha! Good one." He turned that broad body to fully face her and looked her over from head to toe in the yellowy glow of the bar's outside light. "It's really not a bad place."

"What?" Her thoughts were still on what to say to Bruno. "Oh. I'm sure it's fine."

"The beer is a little weak, but the mixed beverages pack a wallop."

The last thing she needed was alcohol. The one thing she *wanted* was exactly that—a stiff drink. It might take the edge off the pain. Allow her to forget the stinkhole of her life. "I'm fine."

His gaze said, *sure you are, buttercup,* but he didn't call her out on it. "You looking for someone?"

She glanced at his keen eyes. A broody gray-blue. Then, realizing she liked them, she self-consciously returned her focus to the door. Military. She could tell by his directness, the way he stood with feet planted. More than that, the energy he gave off. She couldn't describe it, but she always recognized those who'd served, whether they were active duty or vets.

Extrasensory perception, her grandmother had always claimed. "Use it to live your life," she'd told her. "It'll make things easier for you."

No ESP needed in this case. It was an accurate guess simply because of the bar and the fact the vets gravitated here.

Josie had been ignoring her grandmother's words for years, but maybe the old gal was right. Here she was, with nothing but her bullheadedness and handful of woe-is-me. Maybe it was time.

Right now, it was telling her to be truthful with the man. "My brother," she confided. "He's inside and I need to talk to him."

Military faced the door again, his arm only a few inches from hers as he leaned his backside on the railing. "Ahh. So why the hesitation?"

Right. *Let me open up that book of dysfunction.* "Family matters. You know."

At least, she could appreciate that he wasn't standing in front of her anymore, bearing down on her with that...intensity. Now, it was as if he were a companion, a friend.

Don't kid yourself, JJ.

Her so-called friends weren't worth the pins in her leg.

Hell, those were worth way more, come to think of it.

She sensed more than saw his nod. "I have a couple brothers," he told her.

Nothing else, and that was...nice. It sort of said it all – as if that created a bond between them, explaining how they could be. The good and the bad.

Her tense muscles relaxed slightly. She leaned into the railing, too, her shoulder barely brushing his. "He's a great guy, my brother. He deserves a better sister."

The man didn't respond. That was nice as well. No judgment, no empty platitudes. Just that ongoing solidarity.

"Would it be easier if I found him and asked him to come out here?"

She thought about that. "That's considerate of you, and yeah, that might be, but..."

Silence fell like a lead weight. Why was it so damn hard for her to accept help? "I just...I need to do this on my own. Walk in there. Face him. Yeah..."

Another ton of ear-deafening silence. Is that even a thing?

She'd read it in a thriller last night and wondered how it could seem so...loud. Now, she knew.

Her argument sounded lame, even to her own ears. The rejection of his aid also seemed a wee bit bitchy.

Yep, that's me. I epitomize that term these days.

She hadn't always been like this, she reminded herself. Hadn't always been so hard on herself. Full of pain and disappointment.

She'd get back to being *that* Josie—the carefree, fun-loving version—one of these days. Damn straight.

"No problem," Military said, cutting the tension. He pushed off to a standing position. "You think about it. I can come back and check on you in a few minutes. See if you changed your mind."

"You come here often?" she blurted without even thinking, suddenly desperate to make conversation with someone. Anyone.

Someone like him who didn't know all her issues, all her problems.

"Yeah," he admitted, his jean-clad butt hitting the railing again. "My buddy owns the place. I know the majority of patrons, since I'm here a lot." He ran a hand over his mouth. "Not to mention my proclivity for putting my fist into a few of their faces."

Big word that. Apparently, there was a brain behind the brawn.

The last part had been said under his breath, as if he didn't want her to hear it. "What?"

A patron came out, the music clear for a moment, before the door slammed shut again. The guy nodded to Military, who returned it. "Nothing. If your brother is a regular, I know him. It's no problem to locate him and tell him to get his ass out here."

She canted so she could get a better look at him. Had to be over six foot, probably weighed two-twenty or more. There was a scar through his left brow, and if she were betting on her ESP, she'd guess he was a Marine.

"I can handle it." She forced herself to her feet. "But I do appreciate your willingness to help, rosebud."

He grinned and tipped an invisible cap at her. "Always happy to come to the aid of a damsel in distress."

God, he was annoying. She almost yearned for that cane in the car to smack him with.

"Come on," He levered himself upright and opened the door to usher her inside. "Face your demons and all that bull-shit, right?"

She had plenty of those. Gritting her teeth, she forced her leg to cooperate as best as it could, relieved when the joints actually engaged and she only limped slightly across the threshold and into the bar.

The place was noisy and smelled like beer and men. There were a few women here and there, but they were mostly servers. The majority of booths and tables were occupied, big screen TVs showing soccer, football, basketball, and one with a local newscast. Pool tables, pinball machines, and darts—typical setup.

A bruiser of a guy behind the bar raised a hand, and her companion reciprocated. Someone off to the right shouted, "Cahill, get your ass over here."

The man acknowledged the call before shifting to her again. "Caleb Cahill." He held out a hand. "If you need anything, buttercup, I'll be over with that group of jarheads."

Bingo. Marine. She accepted the handshake, enjoying his warm, rough skin. The shake was firm and direct, just as he was, but his touch lingered a second too long before his fingers trailed away.

A spark lit his eyes that took her by surprise, and he kept on staring at her. The air in her lungs caught. It'd been a long time since a guy had looked at her that way, touched her with any type of sensuality.

Military—Caleb—had that in spades.

She found her mouth dry and had to clear her throat. "Thank you," she said. "Again, I appreciate it, but hopefully I won't need further assistance."

Another salute as he backed away a couple steps, nearly crashing in to one of the waitresses. His quick reflexes righted the gal and the tray she carried without spilling a drop.

Smart, sexy, and light on his feet.

Josie found herself smiling.

Damn, another surprise. The ice in her heart was still a solid block, but was she finally coming out of the numbness that Jacob—*the prick*—caused when he broke up with her?

Good, she told herself. It was about damn time.

She enjoyed feeling like a woman. Regardless of her hip, she was attractive, smart, and her independence was a boon, not a weight around her neck.

Right now? Sure, she was a hot mess, but it did her good to know a big, brawny, Marine saw her as more than some limping, exasperated, down-on-her-luck person.

She watched as he sauntered to the group in the far booth. *Turn around*, she thought. *Look back at me.*

But he didn't, and some of that good feeling dribbled out of her. Maybe he was being nice, nothing more.

Or perhaps she was so desperate for attention from a handsome guy she was reading more in to it than there was.

With a heavy sigh, Josie deep-sixed Caleb Cahill and scanned the bar. Where was Bruno?

Biting her bottom lip, she wished for the life of her she could be anywhere else but here.

TWO

That smile.

Caleb watched the woman, whose name he'd failed to get, as she scanned the place again. Her long brown hair was pulled up in a ponytail, the loose pants she wore unable to camouflage the limp she was struggling hard to cover as she made her way around several tables and looked toward the pool table section.

Those dark brown peepers had nearly done him in, and she was nowhere near his type.

As Malachi, his twin, ranted about the basketball team and the score playing above Caleb's head, Caleb kept his focus on her as she drew out her phone and appeared to be texting some-one. Probably this brother of hers.

Caleb wondered if the guy existed. Maybe he wasn't her sibling, but her ex, or even her current boyfriend.

Whoever he was, Caleb suspected he was going to be in for it. While the woman was soft-spoken and had few words to say, he'd gotten the impression she was no pushover, and maybe even a bit of a ball buster.

That big, ugly soft spot in his chest made it hard not to track her as she pocketed the cell and kept scanning the place. She was in trouble, that he was sure of, and like he'd told her outside, he had a thing for damsels in distress.

He'd been teasing, trying to rile her up with the comment. Fact was, she was no weakling and probably didn't need his help, but a part of him couldn't let her go.

"Caleb." Malachi snapped his fingers in front of his face. "You with us?"

Caleb smacked his hand away. "I'm just not into the game. We should shoot some pool."

His other brother, Joe, sitting next to Malachi, looked over his shoulder toward the area where Caleb had been staring. "Who's the woman?"

If only he knew. "Just a gal looking for her brother."

Malachi poured a beer from the pitcher and shoved it toward him, uninterested in the subject. "I thought Bruno was meeting us here tonight."

Joe twisted again, scanning the room more intently. "He better be hunting down DeJon and bringing his worthless ass to us before Friday."

Kevan DeJon had given them the slip more than once in the past month and they'd put Bruno full-time on the halfwit's trail.

Caleb took a long drink, noting the woman had disappeared from view. He shifted in the seat, craning his neck in order to try to find her again. "We should definitely play pool. Table just opened up."

Malachi stretched his arms over his head and smirked. "Is that where your lady friend is? By the tables?"

Caleb rose, downing half the glass as he did so. "I feel like playing, okay? Don't make a thing out of it."

As he walked away, he heard them exchange comments

about the fact that pool had become a code word for bagging women.

"Crass," Caleb called over his shoulder.

Granted, he was a bit of a player and deserved that little dig. Correction—he had been. Those days were over.

The three brothers frequented Bad Medicine on an almost nightly basis. Joe not so much, now that he had Sam in his life, but sometimes even she came with them to blow off steam at the end of a tough day. She was now employed by the SCVC Taskforce, and on occasion, they and the Brothers Bondsmen Agency crossed paths and worked together to bring in fugitives.

Right now, Caleb envied Joe and his marriage. Those two were destined to be, no doubt about it, and Caleb felt a tickle of yearning.

As he made his way through the crowd, several guys reached out to shake his hand or bump his fist. He tried to ignore the jealousy over Joe's happily-ever-after shit. He wasn't one to settle down, never had been, and didn't plan to start any time soon.

Which usually led to flirting with a beautiful woman here or there and following it up with some fun. What was wrong with that? He'd been careful, and he made sure they felt appreciated and had enjoyed themselves as much as he did come sunrise.

It had taken a while, but he'd learned that having a partner in his bed hadn't put out the rage and grief burning inside him. Nothing did anymore.

As he passed the giant antique bar, Dane, called out. "Need another round already?"

"Nah. We're good."

As he moved to the left, he caught sight of the woman and stopped dead in his tracks. She stood near the bathroom hall, but now she looked pissed.

Apparently, her brother was AWOL. She'd seemed so sure outside, Caleb wondered what was going on. Was the creep dodging her? Had he seen her coming in and escaped out the back?

An itch between his shoulders made him wiggle his head to loosen his neck muscles. Rotten bastard. He doubted very much that this man was her brother, and assumed the reason she was searching for him was one of two things: he'd run out on her or cheated on her. Caleb heard about that kind of crap all the time, and if he caught up with whoever this guy was? He'd make sure she got her justice.

Although he tried to keep it under lock and chain, he had a short trigger. He'd been a boxer in college and continued on in the Marines. Might have been a better career for him.

There was something inside him—a kind of rage his brothers didn't have. It made him want to punch people on a regular basis. He'd seen therapists and tried to get to the bottom of it, even going to some energy healer to fix his chakras, whatever the hell those were, to make his mom happy. Nothing worked. No amount of hitting, dealing with his anger over what had happened to his two best friends when he was stationed in Serbia, or any of the pills the doctors ordered to suppress it. He was like the Hulk, angry all the time.

He just didn't know why.

His feet were moving before his mind caught up. She saw him approach and pocketed her phone. She acted almost embarrassed, as if she were going to head to the restroom to avoid him.

A female dodging *him*? Had hell frozen over?

"Hey," he called across the distance. "No luck?"

Like a rabbit caught in a trap, she resumed her stance and shook her head, still not meeting his eyes. He closed in, not sure exactly what he was doing. After all, she told him repeatedly she didn't need his assistance. He didn't know why he wanted to come to her rescue, but hell be a beautiful buttercup, he did.

He gave her his most charming smile. "As long as you're here, you might as well enjoy something more fun than hunting down your brother. I recommend a double shot of tequila, or maybe you like one of those fancier drinks...chocolate martini or...?"

She made a face. "I will never understand why anyone would desecrate chocolate with vodka. The other however, I can get on board with."

"Great. I'll order for us."

Her shoulders slumped. "Unfortunately, I can't. I thought maybe he was in the bathroom, but I've texted him three times and he hasn't responded."

On the left, a handful of guys were whacking pool balls around. Someone cranked up another song on the jukebox. The cacophony of noise, mixed with the talking and laughing, made it hard to have a decent conversation. "Not to sound insensitive, but do you think he went out the back when he saw you coming?"

The woman tilted her head, giving him an odd look. "We aren't super close, but if anything, he'd come running to me, arms thrown wide, asking me what was wrong. He's not one to ignore his little sister, more like smother me."

Caleb's assumptions about the guy changed. She was being truthful. "Can I get you a glass of ice water then? Coffee?"

Her gaze slid to the bar, eyeing a stool, and he could read her mind—she needed to get off that leg, and she was thirsty. "I guess it can't hurt to wait a minute or two and see if he shows."

Caleb wanted to touch her, take her elbow to guide her, but he sensed that'd be the wrong move.

Besides, where was this leading? Nowhere good, he

surmised. He motioned with his free hand. "One ice water coming up."

So as not to call attention to her limp or make her feel more self-conscious, he tried to walk with her, not behind. When a very drunk Lewis – active duty Navy – accidentally lost his balance and knocked in to her, Caleb's reflexes were quick and accurate. He grabbed the prick with a hand, pulling the guy away from her, and steadied her with the other at the same time. His actions kept her from falling in to a table of men playing poker.

"Lewis, you need coffee and sleep." He handed him over to his buddies. "He's had enough. Get him out of here."

Nods from them and a whine from the prick that made Caleb want to jab him. He turned to the woman instead. "Sorry about that. You okay?"

She nodded, and disengaged herself from his steadying grip. "Fine."

And then her phone must've vibrated in her pocket because she reached for it. "It's him." Her eyes lit as they came up to meet Caleb's. "I need to take it."

"Of course." He helped her to a stool as she answered, then lowered his voice and spoke close to her ear. "I'll just be over there, if you need anything."

She nodded while saying hello to her brother. Moving her lips from the cell, she mouthed, "Thanks again."

Feeling dismissed, he made his way to the table his brothers were at. He grabbed a pool cue and started chalking it. The three of them had played so many times, it was natural and automatic for them to set up the balls, and decide who was going to break. Malachi, of course, who always called dibs since he was the eldest. Being born before Caleb by one minute.

A freakin' minute.

Caleb tried not to stare at buttercup, as she spoke. Who was this guy? If his vehicle was in the lot, why wasn't he in here? Had he hooked up with somebody and left?

Mal broke and several balls fell into the pockets. Caleb stood back, gripping the cue a little too tightly, and trying not to let his imagination run wild. He still hadn't gotten the gal's name, and a new type of anger at himself grew inside. *I'm not letting her get away.*

He set it down. "Be right back," he told them.

Joe snorted a caustic remark, but Malachi didn't care. He leaned over the green and took his next shot.

Caleb was two feet from the bar when a young guy with a tie dye shirt slipped onto the seat next to her. She disconnected her call, her face sour, and didn't even glance at him. He wasn't a regular and appeared about nineteen. He leaned toward her, saying something, and put a hand on her shoulder.

As if a bow string snapped, she went into action. A swift movement knocked it off before she grabbed him by the wrist and flipped him around.

Before Caleb could say "holy shit," the guy was on his knees on the floor.

"This kid bothering you?" he asked.

A change came over her, sudden and intense. She let go, as if he'd suddenly caught fire, and looked around confused.

Her dusky skin tinged pink along her cheeks, and she took a step back, her bad leg sliding on the floor. "Oh, I uh..." She drew a deep breath and stared Caleb firmly in the eyes. "I don't like being touched, and I don't know this creep."

Caleb yanked him up by the back of his shirt, ignoring the complaints issuing from his mouth. He was whining about her breaking his wrist, which clearly she hadn't, and Caleb felt a big smile crease his face. Finally, he could be of real help.

"Get lost," he ordered, shoving him away. "And learn some manners, why don't you?"

Grousing and more complaining ensued, the guy's buddies accepting him back into their ranks and shooting daggers at Caleb.

"You didn't have to do that," the woman said. "I know how to take care of myself."

Caleb held up both hands in an act of surrender. "I can see that. Sometimes guys get a little too wasted, and they take liberties they shouldn't. He's not a usual customer, so I can't tell you who he is or why he's here, other than to get drunk and laid."

"Yeah, well…" She pocketed her phone. A few spectators watching the show returned to their beers and games. "My brother's friend had an issue with his dryer. It broke. He was here, but left with him and went to his place to fix it. That's why he's not here now."

Caleb was slightly surprised she admitted all that, but it made sense. "Sounds like a good guy, your brother."

"The best, really. Well, nice to meet you."

"You didn't get your ice water." God, he sounded lame. "You sure you don't want to take me up on that double tequila? I know where Dane keeps the top of the shelf stuff."

She shook her head, teeth nipping at her bottom lip. She might be saying no, but that lip biting suggested she was actually considering it. "I really should go and give up on this flippin' nuts day."

She definitely didn't want to leave, but he wasn't sure she wanted to stay either. "Been there. Say, I didn't get your name."

"Is that important?"

Playing hard to get, or was she overly paranoid? These days? He couldn't blame her. "Actually, you've kind of made my day, and I just was hoping to put a name with the moment."

She laughed without humor. "Does that line work on most women?"

He grinned. "Honestly, I've never used it on anyone else."

His flirting was met with that somewhat mixed up energy of hers – like she enjoyed it, but didn't want it, all the same. "You can call me JJ."

"I'm sorry you had a suckfest of a day, JJ."

"Me, too." She studied him. "You know that thing about Murphy's Law? I have maxed that baby out. I'm not sure, literally, that there is anything else that can go wrong."

Internally he flinched. There was *always* something more that could go wrong. "Okay, that does it," he told her, motioning her back to the stool. "I'm buying you a drink and I don't want to hear any excuses."

She bit her bottom lip again, as if considering his proposal.

Please don't walk out. "Come on, if you prefer ice water, we'll do that instead."

She chuckled again, and this was the real deal. It brightened her face, and it lit something deep inside him at the same time. "Fine. How about one of each? A single shot of tequila and a double ice water?"

He wasn't sure his grin could grow any bigger, but it did. "You're on."

Just as they were about to resume their seats, the drunk kid came out of nowhere and tackled him.

THREE

One minute, Josie was letting Caleb help her to her seat, the next he crashed in to her and like dominoes, they both went down.

Pain screamed through her hip; his weight crushed the air from her lungs. Her head hit the floor, and in the back of her mind, she cringed, thinking about all the things that had been spilled here. The smell alone was enough to make her gag.

Then, she found herself looking in to those incredible eyes of his, and he shifted immediately. She could breathe again as he eased his glorious, muscled frame off hers.

"Are you hurt?"

She shook her head, not able to find her voice, and locked in his gaze, the rest of the world seemed to pause for a moment. While he was no longer crushing her, she still felt the heat from his delicious body, and the fire she saw in his eyes—a mix of anger and gentleness—nearly undid her.

A few people gathered around them, the jukebox continuing to blare and the knock of cues against pool balls echoing over it. The kid was screaming at them, and over Caleb's shoulder she could see him bouncing on the balls of his feet, fists raised.

His two friends were trying to rein him in, and she noticed the bartender, of all people, smiling as he peered from behind the bar, cleaning a glass. "Never a dull moment," he said over the buzz.

"I'm fine," she lied. Her left foot was tangled in the stool, which apparently had crashed with them and now lay beside her. Her injured leg, currently under Caleb, was surprisingly okay. All she could do was stare in to those orbs, feel the strength and warmth of him surrounding her.

In a flash, he was gone, lifting himself off of her. He reached down and offered a hand, so she grabbed it, allowing him to help her sit up. She didn't like being touched, but with him it was different.

The stupid kid took a swing, and without even looking, Caleb used his free hand to nail the idiot on the side of the head. As the drunk fell, her hero pulled her the rest of the way to her feet.

The noise of the bar suddenly became that of the battle-field. People screaming, cries of pain, the ricochet of bullets.

Sweat broke out along her temple; her pulse raced.

She couldn't breathe.

Everything was blanketed in that haze of the past, her heart triple-timing it, hands trembling like her legs. Her balance was off, and she tripped. Caleb's hands gripped her arms.

His eyes remained locked on hers, and she felt that lifeline go down her spine and anchor her in place. Someone else gripped her shoulders, and she heard the man say, "Stupid a-hole is back up, C."

The anger she'd seen in Caleb flared brighter. "You sure you're okay?"

She nodded hesitantly, pointing over his shoulder at the

boy who was rearing back to swing. Her mouth started to yell, "Look out!" but it wasn't necessary.

Caleb let go of her and became a raging bull.

He tackled the moron, and sent them both to the floor. The bar erupted in a wave of cheers and jeers.

Caleb put a stop to the boy's attack almost as quickly as it started, clocking him upside the head, then a quick jab to the nose. Blood splattered.

Other fights broke out, and the bartender kept polishing the glass as if this were an everyday occurrence.

All this over her? Caleb raised a fist to punch again, and Josie started forward to stop him. The hands on her shoulders gripped tighter, keeping her in place. "You don't want to get in the middle of that," the stranger said.

She glanced at him and saw a striking resemblance to Caleb. He was the guy who called out to them when they'd entered. His hair was slightly darker and he sported several days' worth of beard.

The brother Caleb had mentioned. "He's gonna kill that kid."

"Nah. Teach him a lesson, though."

Another man standing near them made his way through the fighting and yelling patrons. Planting his feet, he heaved Caleb up and shoved him away.

Caleb got in his face and started yelling, but Josie couldn't hear what they were saying because of the chaos. He also looked like Caleb, even more so than the one holding her. Same height, same square jaw, same overall build.

There was blood on Caleb's shirt, his knuckles. Josie cursed Murphy's Law for taking her to even more heights of shittiness.

Out of nowhere, one of the friends came rushing blindly from the throng. He carried a raised beer bottle above him.

On the warpath.

Everything went into slow motion for her.

He was aiming for Caleb. Who was still intently arguing with his brother.

Josie screamed.

The bottle came down on Caleb's head, shattering in a dozen pieces.

He staggered. Grabbed for a chair. It toppled and Caleb nearly fell.

Blood was everywhere. Josie's stomach lurched.

This time, it wasn't only Caleb who went after the attacker. He and his brother grabbed the guy and hauled him away, disappearing into the crowd.

A foghorn noise rang out, and everybody jumped, the raised voices falling to near silence. The bartender stood with the horn at the counter, a patient smile on his face. "Clean this shit up, or I'm kicking all of you out. You'll be banned for three weeks."

"Yes, captain!" Good-naturedly, those around her began to shout apologies and do as ordered. Tables and chairs were straightened. The semi-conscious kid on the floor, nose busted, was escorted to the door. The jukebox could be heard again, the broken glass was cleaned up, and several resumed a pool game.

Within a few heartbeats, the entire place appeared as it had been, only missing a couple patrons.

Josie turned to the man still hanging out with her. "Where'd they go?"

"He'll be back in a minute."

She caught the bartender's attention, leaning on the bar. "This was my fault. I'm so sorry. Please don't kick Caleb out over this."

He barely glanced at her, pouring tequila into two shot glasses, and setting them on the countertop with a napkin. "You don't need to worry about that a-hole," he said. "We're used to his brawling."

The brother with her scanned the bar and nodded.

She steeled herself to ignore the liquor. Her nerves needed it, her stomach did not. "I take it he gets in to a few fights?"

"More than we'd like," the man said and smiled. In it, she saw a reflection of Caleb.

"He's your brother?"

"Unfortunately, yeah."

At that moment, Caleb reappeared, skirting folks until he reached her. He grabbed her hand, rubbing it gently with his thumb. "Sorry about that."

He had a cut on his cheekbone that was bleeding profusely. She grabbed a napkin. "You didn't need to defend my honor like that," she said sarcastically, putting pressure on the injury. "And you're gonna need stitches."

He placed his hand over hers, stilling her efforts. "Just a scratch, buttercup. I'm fine."

She glanced at the bartender. "Tell me you have a first-aid kit."

He was serving a beer to someone down the way, and cocked his head, gesturing to the rear of the building. "Back room, take a left, top shelf."

Pulling her hand from his, she grabbed Caleb by the shirt-sleeve and marched him in that direction to find it.

FOUR

aleb had his own personal Clara Barton.

Better than the famous nurse, in fact. JJ was spectacular, sexy, and beautiful. He sat on the low stool with her stationed between his legs, and as she doctored his cuts, he was in pure heaven.

She was gentle yet firm, intelligent, and didn't take any guff from him.

Bonus, her generous breasts were at eye level. While he'd noticed them earlier, he hadn't paid as much attention because he'd been so caught up in her stunning eyes. Now, there was no getting away from them, and he was a sad sack of shit because he had no desire to stare anywhere else.

"Three or four stitches, max," she claimed, using a cotton swab to layer on antiseptic cream. "You're definitely going to have a scar."

"Just another to add to my collection."

She struggled to stop the flow, but he was quite content — scar or no—to stay right where he was and let her tend him. It came natural to her and he wasn't one to look a gift horse in the mouth.

She capped the tube and tossed it on the table where the kit lay open, its parts scattered. "You're as bullheaded as they come, aren't you?"

Reluctantly, he met her accusatory stare. "A little scratch isn't going to send me running to the emergency room."

Her fingers nimbly rifled through the few items still in the dusty box. "If I had the correct tools, I could do it for you. Unfortunately, this is in need of fresh supplies."

"Are you a nurse?"

Her attention went everywhere but his face. "Was."

A single word, and yet it conveyed a whole lot of emotion. He wanted to ask her what happened, but the loaded tone suggested that would be a bad idea.

She snagged butterfly bandages and more gauze. Using the latter, she cleaned the area around the cut, removing excess cream. Opening the packages, she carefully placed the tiny closures on his skin.

She was mere centimeters from him, and it was all he could do not to lean forward and taste her lips.

"How many brothers do you have?"

He could smell her shampoo, or maybe it was some sort of body wash. The delicate scent of flowers and vanilla tickled his nostrils. He inhaled deeply, soaking it in as he studied her face, so close to his. "Too many."

"All three of you Marines?"

He studied her even closer. "Just two of us. Joe's a wanker and didn't go in to the military. He chose the FBI instead, and that got him a buttload of trouble. How'd you guess?"

The corner of her mouth tugged in to something that passed as a smile. "I have ESP."

She placed another miniature strip like a bridge over his

cut, smoothing it with her fingers. "You have a lot of anger you haven't processed," she said, a statement of fact. "You should see a therapist."

This made him laugh, and she drew back, a frustrated frown present because the move caused her to stick the third bandage in the wrong spot. "So, you're a psychiatrist, too?"

"Hold still." She reapplied it, bringing that beautiful face of hers right in front of his again as she eyed the wound. "I've been on the couch a few times."

"Did it do any good?"

Her eyes met his, and he saw the way they shuttered before she answered, "Not a damn bit, but I'm not you. I don't know what you're carrying around, but that right hook could really hurt somebody one of these days."

She had him there. He'd already done damage to people over the years, but most had been in a ring where they expected it. "The kid's fine. You don't need to worry about his lousy ass."

Finished her work, she took his chin between thumb and finger and moved him as she eyed the smaller cuts. Those were no longer bleeding, thanks to her ministrations, but she scowled anyway. "Let's put some salve on these."

When she went to reach for the cream, he caught her wrist. "I'm fine. We still need to get you that drink."

Those peepers came back to meet his, looking darker with some unexpressed emotion. "Thanks, but I really need to call it a day. I'm dead on my feet, and if one more thing goes wrong..."

Her gaze slid back to the table, but she didn't pull from his grasp. He took his thumb and rubbed it across the delicate skin of her wrist. Her pulse jumped in response. "Thank you. I appreciate the care."

She moved from her spot and he let go of her wrist, wishing he knew the right words to keep her from pulling away from him. He rose to help her collect the items and return them to the container. His mind raced through contingency plans. Anything to get her to stay, to open up.

Her hand brushed his as she reached across to gather the dirty gauze and toss it in the garbage. They continued to work in a comfortable silence, and he was at least glad for that. Everything he came up with seemed inadequate, and he felt like he was sixteen again, struggling to ask a girl out.

He hadn't felt like that in a long, long time. "Hey, I can do this, if you want to get going."

Why the hell had he said that? He was trying to keep her here, not give her more reasons to leave.

She glanced up and jabbed him gently with an elbow. "Now you're trying to get rid of me?"

The grin on her face was half-hearted, but he gave her a big smile in return. He leaned a hip on the table, so he could look her straight in the eye. "I'm actually standing here trying to come up with a reason to make you stay, but I can't find one I think will actually work."

Her expression softened, her hands pausing while repacking. A heavy silence hung between them for a minute.

"Maybe I do need that drink."

Score!

"Whatever you want. I owe you."

"Huh," was all she said in response.

Out at the bar, he helped her on to the stool, noting she was favoring that leg again. A few moments later, Dane had drinks in front of them and Caleb was glad to see Malachi and Joe were still playing pool.

Not that he expected differently. The way they were eyeing him, he knew he'd get chewed out later, but if this thing with JJ went south, he'd need a few rounds of hitting balls himself.

He might even have to stop at the gym on the way home and take some of his frustration out on the punching bag.

"How long are you on leave, rosebud?"

Her question brought him back to the present, pushing thoughts of losing this mission right out of his mind. No retreat. No surrender.

"Permanently." He downed a gulp of beer. "Retired."

"Ah. Did you enjoy it? Being in?"

"Sure." Best to keep it light. No way he'd admit that the simple fact of seeing his own blood brought flashbacks of what happened in his final days.

The irony always hit him fresh when he thought about the fact that he was constantly in the MMA ring, beating people to a pulp and getting his ass kicked at the same time, blood flying everywhere. Yet, after it was over, and he saw it on his own hands and face, the PTSD would sometimes come roaring back like a monster coming out of the closet.

She hit him with another probing question. "Hard being a civilian again?"

No way was he going to admit any of that, and especially not with this skittish colt sitting next to him. "Nah. Helps having my brothers. They keep me straight, even when they piss the hell out of me."

It was amazing to see her shoulders relax slightly and a true smile break over her face. "That's what they're for, right?"

They knocked drinks together in a combo touché and cheers. "Oorah," he said, and she laughingly echoed it.

The jukebox song died and the place was relatively normal for a bit. He started to ask her about nursing, knowing it was risking her clamming up again, but then a dinging came from her phone and she glanced at the time on it.

"Oh geez, it's getting late. I've got to go."

She slid off, and he jumped down, still not ready to let her run. "Let me walk you out."

She placed a hand on his arm to stop him. "I had a good time, except for the bar brawl part. I take it you hang out here often?"

"More than I should," he admitted. "Maybe I'll see you again some time?"

Jeez, he sounded desperate.

She went up on her tiptoes and kissed his cheek. "I'd like that."

It was so unexpected, he lost his train of thought, and then she was past him and walking toward the door, that limp telling him she was in pain.

He raised a hand to touch the spot. "Oorah," he murmured and started to go after her.

Joe stepped into his line of sight. "We're starting a new game. You in, *rosebud?*"

Shit, just like Joe to be eavesdropping. Fucking Fed.

He brushed past and then had to dodge around a group of drunken guys, staggering toward the jukebox.

By the time he got to the door, JJ was across the parking lot and heaving herself into an old beat-up Durango.

Night had fallen, and the SUV was in partial shadows. When she turned the key, the bucket of rust made a whining sound, choked, and died.

He stopped on the top step and watched as she tried again. Got the same result.

She slid out, slamming the door, and shuffling to the front to raise the hood. As she did so, one of the kids from the earlier brawl slunk from the shadows.

"Hey, bitch. My boy has a broken nose, thanks to you. I think a little compensation is in order."

Caleb was down and running, but he needn't worry. JJ

reached out, grabbed the kid's button-down collar, and yanked him forward. At the same time, she hefted a knee and jammed it in his groin.

Keeping hold of his shirt as his knees buckled, she leaned closer and said something low in his ear. Then she shoved him to the gravel.

He groaned in pain, clutching the injured appendage. Weakly, he kicked out at her.

She limped to the vehicle, opened the back hatch and returned with a tire iron. Caleb stopped, a grin spreading across his face.

"You better start crawling," she told the kid, pointing at his abdomen. "If you ever get in my space again, there's gonna be a whole lot more than a broken nose between you and your pals."

Still in pain, the SOB came up on hands and knees and began crawling. She smacked the makeshift weapon into her open palm a couple times, watching him go.

Caleb stayed where he was, hooking his thumbs into his belt loops. "Car trouble, buttercup?" At her exasperated eyeroll, he laughed. "Sounds like the carburetor."

She glanced at the engine. "That, timing belt, I think the head gasket is about to explode, and a few other minor things like the starter."

"You either need a ride, or a completely new car."

"I'll call my brother."

He dug his keys out of his pocket and held them up in the glow of the light. "I can take you wherever you need."

She bit her bottom lip, and he almost groaned like the kid had, because damn, he wanted to kiss it and wipe that frustration off her face. "The thing is, you really can't."

She was a ballbuster and seemed determined to kill him, right here and now. Why was it so hard for her to accept a little help?

Good thing he was as stubborn as they came. "All right then." He tossed the keys in the air. "Take my truck."

She caught them with ease and stared at him dumbfounded. "What?"

He pointed at the copper colored F150 under the palm tree a few feet away. "When you're done with it, return it here and leave the keys with Dane."

He turned on his heel to walk back to the bar and was rewarded when she called after him, "Are you out of your mind? You don't even know me and you're giving me your ride?"

He stopped at the bottom of the steps to grin at her. "I have a form of ESP, too. I know what kind of person you are, and I'm not worried. Take it, go home. Bring it here tomorrow, or whenever. I trust you."

He turned toward the building again. Everything he'd said was true. He *did*, for some crazy reason, even with his precious baby.

"Caleb?"

He was halfway up and he stopped, his fingers on the railing as he swiveled. "Yeah?"

She just stared at him, saying nothing for a long moment. Then she tossed the tire iron down, before she walked across the parking lot, her injured leg no longer seeming to bother her so much. She hoisted herself up the stairs, a fierce look on her face.

He braced for a chewing out. She opened her mouth, but snapped it shut again. "I don't understand you."

He grinned down at her. "Not many do."

The next thing he knew, she reached out, grabbed him by the back of the neck, and brought her lips to his.

FIVE

"I thought you had to get home."

His voice was teasing. Josie slid the back of her hand across her lips. She did, but...

The kiss had set off fireworks low inside her.

As Caleb grinned, she thought about smacking him.

Instead, she grabbed his shirt and tugged. "Stress relief. I'm going to explode and no amount of alcohol will take the edge off."

Off the steps they went, Josie gritting her teeth against the stiffness in her leg. "You game or not, rosebud?"

His laugh came from his belly. Next thing she knew, his arms went around her and her body was lifted from the ground.

Caleb carried her across the gravel. All she could do was hold on. "Buttercup, I am *always* game."

The inside of the truck was kitted out with all the latest gadgets. The soft leather was welcome against her skin, cool and inviting, as he gently kissed her onto her back, his fingers rubbing the waist of her jeans.

Damn, what was she doing?

Good at the game of compartmentalizing, she slammed the door shut on her inner saint and opened the one for her sinner.

Caleb's lips trailed to her jaw, her earlobe. His teeth slid down her neck to her collarbone and he nibbled the sensitive area of her shoulder, pushing her tank strap off.

He was warm and strong, but gentle, taking it slow, teasing her. Lazy almost, his mouth doing things to her that made her arch, grip his shoulders, and call his name.

Not only was he good with his fists, he was with his fingers, too. When he put the two together to work on her, she was gone. "Let go, JJ. I won't hurt you."

She expected a quickie, hadn't planned to even fully remove her pants. Instead, she found herself naked and at his mercy, the shadows of the parking lot hiding the truck and their indecency.

After covering himself with a condom, he shifted her over him, his incredible strength and gentleness lowering her into a comfortable position on top.

She stared at his battle-scarred body, similar to and yet so different from her own. The need to know where they'd come from filled her, but the desperate ache to get him inside her won out.

"Time to stop thinking," he said, his voice thick with the same need.

Slick and ready, she enveloped his erection, her hands braced on his hard pecs. He made encouraging noises, gripping her hips, supporting her as his own moved to meet her.

When she was fully seated with him buried deep, she let her head fall back, absorbing the moment. Her bad hip no longer existed. Her bad luck, either. She could let go of the shame and anger, and simply be a woman making love to a man.

The escape from her life was welcome and the core of her

desire made her body move on its own in an ancient rhythm. *No more thinking.*

Just feeling.

Sensations racked her as Caleb coaxed her along. He met every stroke, every shift. "That's right. Let yourself go."

She did, and soon felt the release coming.

Too soon.

But she couldn't stop or slow down.

She needed it. That bliss.

Needed the man under her.

The tempo, the throb and pulse, became faster, harder. Caleb palmed her breasts, massaging them, raising to lick one then the other as her walls contracted.

She gasped. "Jesus!"

"Close, but not quite," he teased.

He kept her moving, wringing every last wave of the climax from her. As she floated in the pleasure, his muscles tightened and his face contorted.

"Fuck, buttercup," he ground out as his orgasm struck, his hips bucking under hers. "You're so damn...beautiful."

The last word came out like a prayer.

She smiled to herself, eventually shifting to lay her head on his chest. Listening to his strong heartbeat, she closed her eyes and drifted.

TWO HOURS later and fully satiated, Josie waved to Caleb as she drove out of the lot, and immediately shut off the built-in GPS tracking system.

No one could know where she was hanging out. Not her knight in shining armor, not her brother. No. One.

The abandoned airfield came into view thirty minutes later,

the deepest part of the night plastered with a star-filled sky. She parked in a secluded area and hiked the short distance to the main building, using a break in the fence to slip through.

A few random lights picked up the glowing eyes of feral cats moving in the black shadows. Some realized their meal ticket had arrived and cried, following her inside.

She fed them and put two bowls out for the truly wild cats who wouldn't allow her close to them. In the office she'd designated as her bedroom, her cell buzzed.

Bruno was on the other end. "Sorry again, sis."

"It's fine. Can you see if your friend can do anything with my car?"

"I got it started and drove to the garage. Should hear back in a day or so. Where are you?"

"My place." It wasn't exactly a lie. "Don't worry, I called for a ride. Heading to bed now."

"Okay, get some sleep. I'll pick you up in the morning."

"For what?"

"The office manager position, remember? They'll hire you on the spot, guaranteed."

Right, she'd forgotten with everything else going on. She was never going to dig herself out of the hole she was in if she didn't get a job. "Beggars can't be choosers, right?"

"Once you're back in fighting shape, you can return to nursing. This is a nice place to work. Plus, you'll get to see me every day."

She smiled at the cheekiness in his voice. "Text me the address. I'll get a ride and meet you there."

"It's no problem for me to pick you up."

Except it was. "You're an amazing big brother, but it *is* out of your way, and I can call the service. Stop hovering. I promise I'll be there by nine, cool?"

A heavy sigh nearly knocked her over from the guilt. "See you then."

Phew. She hated arguing with him. He could be so bull-headed. Not that she wasn't. "I love you, big B."

"I love you, too, little J."

SIX

The next morning, Caleb's cheek was stiff from the swelling and his ears ached from Malachi giving him grief over the bar fight.

Joe seemed more upset about him hooking up with JJ in the lot, and then giving her his truck.

As Caleb searched for a fresh can of coffee, Joe filled the carafe with water. "I thought you gave that up."

"The brawling?" He shrugged, slamming the cabinet where it should've been and wasn't. "I didn't instigate it."

"You didn't walk away from it, either." Joe emptied the contents into the coffee maker. "And you got sucked into all of it because you can't think with your big brain instead of your pitiful small one."

"My dick is twice the size of yours, Fed boy." Just thinking about JJ and her amazing body made his shoulders unkink. For the good part of two hours, he'd stopped beating himself up. The rage and the grief he carried like a hundred-pound weight had disappeared. "Besides, it was worth it."

He'd had every intention of being with her, his own

personal Clara Barton, but he'd been set to let her leave. Then she'd kissed him. All bets were off at that point.

That had made his brain go on the fritz. He'd stopped feeling like a bomb ready to go off and started feeling...

He'd thought about it all night. What exactly had he felt when JJ kissed him?

Horny, sure, but something else. Something...

Soft. Peaceful.

He felt strong without even throwing a punch. Like his old self. "I was just doing my civic duty. She needed help."

Joe snickered, opening a cabinet to help in the search. "You don't even know her name."

"Do, too. It's JJ."

"JJ what?"

Oh hell. "What do you care, Joe? It's my goddamn life."

"I thought you were done with the one-night stands."

Just because his younger brother was married, he was suddenly an expert on relationships. "Not all of us are lucky like you," he sneered. "And neither one of us is going to be if we don't find the damn coffee."

Malachi sauntered in, snagging one of his health drinks from the fridge. "You guys used the last of the coffee yesterday, remember?"

"Shit." Joe slammed the cabinet door. "I'll run to the convenience store and grab some."

Out in the front office, the bell over the door jingled. Malachi pointed at Caleb. "You're running the interviews for the secretary position today. Get someone hired."

"I'm injured." Caleb pointed at his cheek and made a sad face. "Can't you do it?"

Malachi gave him the stink eye, a glare that would make a lesser man piss himself, before walking out. "Suck it up. And go shave."

Damn. No wonder he'd made sergeant.

He tapped a fist, his bruised knuckles complaining, against the counter. *Joe better hurry.*

Scratching his beard, he entertained the idea that maybe whoever was out front needed to post bail and the paperwork would keep him busy all morning.

What's the matter with me? Since when did he actually hope for that? He hated the damn stuff.

Which was why they needed a secretary.

Caleb trailed after his older-by-a-minute twin, yearning to be out hunting down one, if not all, of the skip traces listed on the whiteboard. It wasn't a new client waiting for him, though. It was only Bruno.

Malachi sipped his disgusting green drink and pointed at Caleb. "He's doing the interviews today."

Bruno Jackson was a beefy SOB who lived and breathed loyalty to the Marines, and more importantly, to the bail bonds business. Six-foot-four and dressed all in leather from head to toe, the earrings and tats he proudly displayed suggested he was more of a thug than a bounty hunter. "Hey, man."

"Yo. Catch DeJon yet?"

A shake of his head. "You remember about my sister, right?"

Caleb searched his memory, which was more than a little fuzzy without his morning caffeine. "The one who moved here from L.A. last month? What about her?"

"Don't dick with me, bro. The interview." Bruno's dark gaze shot daggers at him. "She's competent and reliable, just down on her luck."

Caleb sorted through several stacks of folders. They needed help in the worst way, after their previous assistant had bailed on them once her fiancé came back from his last tour of duty. They hadn't found a suitable replacement yet, mostly because none of them had been seriously trying. "I'm sure she's great."

Bruno leaned on the desk, his evil warlord look firmly in place. "I told Mal she'd be stopping by."

Business was booming, and every guy on the roster had two or three cases they were working, as evidenced by the large board behind him. "To apply for the desk job?"

"She's not exactly bounty hunter material." He eyed Caleb's split cheek. "Although, damn it, she'll take one look at you and want to fix you, sure as shit."

"There's no fixing me," Caleb told him, now searching through a drawer.

Joe had taken two more skips, while Malachi was barely keeping up with the paperwork. Caleb himself had been on the street multiple times in the last few weeks, which was cool with him, chasing down a gal who hadn't shown up for her bail arraignment.

"I want your word that you'll keep your hands off her," Bruno said.

"Why would I touch your sister?"

"She's a beauty and..."

Caleb straightened. "And what? You think I jump every pretty girl who comes along?"

Malachi's voice echoed from the back. "Don't answer that!"

Caleb went back to sorting. Bruno put both fists down and leaned forward, trying to catch Caleb's eye. "She's *my baby sister*. We clear?"

His tone made Caleb pause and squint at the guy. "Are you threatening me, B? You do remember I'm your boss, right?"

Bruno turned his head and spit on the floor. "Family is family. You lay one finger on her and I'll..."

"Gross man. Clean that up."

"I know, I know." Badass Bruno morphed into softhearted

teddy bear. He grabbed a tissue from the box on the desk. "I'm sorry, man, but I can't stand the thought of anyone messing with her head, you know? She's got enough issues as it is."

This morning Caleb needed a file on Carmen Luca, and hell if he knew where it was. He shifted a pile of manila folders, craning his head to read the side tabs. "Look, as long as she has two hands and can answer the phone" – which started ringing as if on cue – "she's hired."

The bell over the door bing-bonged and Joe entered, two cans of coffee in hand. He headed for the kitchenette, and Bruno leaned his bulky frame onto the desk. "She can do more than that, I promise you. She's no slouch."

"Great. Aha!" Caleb spotted what he needed and jerked it out of the pile, sending several others skittering to the floor. "Damn it. When she gets here, get her some coffee and bring her to my office."

He did a half-hearted job of collecting the scattered items and tossing them back on the desktop. Hopefully Bruno's sister was organized, 'cause, jeez what a mess.

As he made his way down the east hall to his office, he heard Bruno call. "Here she is now."

At his desk, he made himself open the folder and take out the original application Carmen's mother had filled out. Sure enough, he found the phone number he needed, and was about to dial, when he heard the front bell go off again. Malachi had snagged the caller, and the first few wafts of coffee trickled past his nose.

Hiring the new secretary would be a breeze if all he had to do was check out Bruno's sister and give her the green light.

Perhaps this day wouldn't be shit after all.

And just maybe, he'd get the chance to track down JJ and find out what kind of trouble she was truly in.

She'd been smart enough to disable the GPS, but he had other ways of finding her.

A woman's hushed voice argued with Bruno out front. Bits and pieces of the conversation filtered in to him, Bruno trying to convince her that this was a good job and would help her get back on her feet.

Caleb rubbed a hand over his face, trying to concentrate on the call he needed to make. He wrote the number on a sticky note and stuck it on his phone, flipping through several pages in the folder on Carmen.

His phone rang and a glance at the landline showed Mal was still on the other call. Joe, the bastard, never answered the phone. He grabbed the handset just as Bruno appeared in the doorway, a goofy smile on his face.

"Caleb, I want you to meet my sister."

Bruno stepped in, leaving the doorway vacant. Caleb paused in pushing the button to take the call, waiting for Bruno's sister to appear, but all he saw was empty hallway space beyond the door.

He shot a look at Bruno, whose smile fell off his face. The big man stepped back to the frame, looking around into the hall. "Josie!"

No answer. Nobody appeared.

Bruno gave him an embarrassed grin and left.

Caleb answered and woke up his computer. He didn't have time for games. Either she wanted the job or she didn't.

Please let her want it. "Bondsman Brothers. Ass in a jam? We've got your plan."

He tucked the receiver between his shoulder and ear as he typed, responding to the person about the fact that yes, they did have to show up in person for their bail hearing.

He was reading the screen in front of him, tuning out the whining on the other end of the line, when he caught movement out of the corner of his eye. Bruno and his sister re-entered the office, and Bruno leaned forward waving to get Caleb's attention.

He held up a finger, finished the conversation, and plunked the handset back on the unit, without looking at either of them, still perusing the information that he needed.

"Caleb." Bruno waved a hand toward the woman next to him. "I want you to meet my pride and joy. This is my baby sister, Josie."

"Oh my god," the woman said, and the hairs on the back of his neck stood at attention.

Slowly, almost afraid of what he might see, he slid his gaze from the computer. As it landed on her, his pulse went all kinds of haywire, and so did his dick.

She was dressed in a simple black shirt and pants. Conservative and...well, secretarial, he guessed.

But the fire in her glare? The bright flush on her cheeks? That was all JJ.

"You have got to be kidding," she ground out.

"Hello, buttercup." He leaned back in the chair. "We meet again."

"What fresh hell is this?"

Josie was pretty sure she was either cursed or had some bad, bad karma biting her in the ass from the way her week was going.

"You two know each other?" Bruno asked, shocked.

There was no way Caleb from last night could be the guy her brother told her about in need of a secretary. "You said somebody named Malachi was the owner," she mumbled. "That's the only person you ever mentioned."

Caleb raised a brow at Bruno and put a hand on his chest. "Really, bro? You never told her about me?"

Bruno gave a derisive snort, then looked down his broad nose at her. "Where'd you meet him? Did he...do anything?"

She scrunched up her face. "Stop it. Right. Now. Nothing other than help me out, which"—she put her hands on her hips—"is more than you did."

Behind the desk, Caleb was staring at them with a bemused expression on his face. The phone rang and he reached for the handset, knocking it askew. He fumbled to put it back in the cradle, but it didn't quite fit and went tumbling off to the side.

"Never mind." She patted Bruno on the shoulder. "I'll show myself out."

"Damn it." Caleb slammed the handset down and the ringing stopped.

"What?" Bruno reached for her. "Wait!"

Caleb stood, rocketing out of his chair. "Don't go, JJ."

The phone rang again, and he snatched up the black plastic then put it right back down. In the process, he managed to knock the landline so hard, it jumped, colliding into a stack of files.

Attempting to stop them from toppling, he got his fingers caught in the cord, yanking it and causing the entire mess to go flying, spreading over the floor like 52-card pickup.

Josie paused as Caleb swore again, her brother looking between them with a hard frown. "Did you just call her JJ?"

Caleb stopped and pinned her with a look. She stood her ground and returned it. Awkward.

"You're hired," Caleb said untangling his fingers. "Can you start today? Like, right now?"

Josie searched for any hint of deception. What must be going through his mind? The way her luck was a Murphy's Law disaster, he probably only wanted to hire her because he assumed she'd be an easy fuck buddy. "I think that would be a bad idea, don't you?"

Bruno's focus narrowed as he continued to ping-pong between them. "What did I warn you about?"

This seemed to be directed at Caleb.

Caleb raised both hands in the air. "Like your sister said, I helped her, that's all."

"Your boss got into a fight." She wondered what torture Bruno must have promised to inflict if Caleb *did anything to her*. Was it any wonder she rarely even had a date growing up? Her bruiser of a sibling was always threatening them. Didn't take ESP to know he'd been defending her honor in place of their no-good father, who'd run out on them when she was only two. "I was there."

"At the bar?" Bruno queried.

She patted his shoulder again. "He filled in for you, defending me against a young kid who tried to make trouble. I felt bad about it, and he managed to cheer me up."

She saw the twitch of Caleb's lips at her phrasing and blasted him with another fierce glare.

Bruno sized them both up and pointed at Caleb's injured cheek. "She did that, didn't she? Cleaned you up?"

Caleb nodded. "And for that, I'm indebted to her." He glanced her way. "Please stay. We are desperate, and if you're willing to work with him, the rest should be a piece of cake."

Regardless of the tense situation, that made her laugh. She punched Bruno in his muscled arm. "Think he's got your number, big brother."

Bruno put an arm around her shoulders, all serious. "You don't have to, you know. You can move in with me."

It was a terrible idea—accepting this job—but it was worse thinking about mooching off her brother.

He was always trying to take care of her, even now. She smiled and patted his cheek. "I don't need a handout, just a paycheck, but thank you. I appreciate the offer."

Bruno hugged her and over his shoulder, she saw Caleb smirk. He winked at her, like they had a secret.

They did, but she wanted to knock it right off. Especially because it triggered memories from the previous night. Heat started low in her belly and wormed its way down her legs. She remembered his lips on her neck, her collarbone, lower...

Releasing her brother, she coughed, and straightened her shirt. *This is never going to work.*

Dammit.

"How is it?" She pointed to Caleb's cheek.

He absentmindedly touched it. "Good as new. You have quite a gift."

Brown noser. The gleam in his eyes told her he was remembering their time together in his truck, too.

This wasn't going to happen, no matter how badly she wanted it to. She'd screwed up her only potential job at the moment for sex.

But she wasn't a pity case, and she wasn't about to be anyone's fuck buddy.

"Nice try." She dug out his keys, tossed them to him, and headed for the door. "Good luck finding someone else."

EIGHT

osie was leaving. He had to stop her. Now.

"Hey!" Caleb scrambled from around his desk, pushing Bruno out of the way. "Don't leave yet. Let's talk about it."

As he hit the waiting room, a woman entered, crying. She looked at Josie who stopped next to the desk. "My baby. He's being framed. I need help."

Josie peeked at Caleb as he swore softly under his breath. Just what he needed. "I'll be with you in a moment, ma'am. Have a seat."

She ignored him, reaching out to Josie. "The judge set bail at five thousand dollars. I don't know how this works. I need money to get him out of there. He'll never survive lockup!"

She began weeping and Josie accepted her hand.

The Good Samaritan.

Joe popped in to see what the noise was about, and Bruno came up behind Caleb. They all watched as Josie led her over to one of the upholstered seats and sat next to her, never letting loose. "What's your son's name?"

The woman drew a tissue from her pocket and sniffled in to it. "Emmanuel. He's all I've got in this world. He would never do what they said he did."

Josie patted her arm. "I need you to take a deep breath for me. We're going to get this figured out, okay?"

Joe shot Caleb a frown, turned on his heel, and fled like the hounds of hell were after him.

Coward.

"What's your name?" Josie asked the woman.

"Udela."

Bruno look flustered, going behind the desk, as if he knew what to do to take her information and set up the bail. That was a joke since Bruno was as disorganized as you could get. His saving grace was the fact he could run down any fugitive or skip trace and bring them in.

Caleb shooed Bruno out of the way and located a clipboard. While Josie calmed the woman, getting her to talk about Emmanuel, he rifled through a drawer and found the intake form. Securing it, he handed both to Josie with a pen.

"Okay, Udela. Let's take down some details." She accepted the items. Step by step, she asked the questions on the form, and around Udela's sobs, was able to get the pertinent facts.

As Bruno leaned on the desk, watching, Caleb sat and booted up the computer. As long as Josie was extracting tidbits from the woman, he would start filling out the online forms.

Within a few minutes they had everything, including the facts regarding Udela's house. She only needed five hundred to handle the ten percent of the bail requirement, but didn't even have that to spare.

Days like this were too numerous and made his anger surface. Some poor slob, who still lived with his mom, was committing petty crimes, getting busted, and making her cover his ass.

Caleb printed the various forms requiring Udela's signature, and Josie played intermediary again. Eventually, they wrapped it up, Udela got what she came for, and Josie walked the woman to the door.

Udela gripped Josie's hands. "Thank you. I was so scared to come here and do this, but you made it so easy."

Bruno snatched a business card from the desk and handed to her. "Call us if you need anything, and make sure Emmanuel shows for his court date."

"I will. I will."

After the door closed behind her, Bruno caught Caleb's eye. "See? She's a natural."

His phone went off and, after checking the screen, he grunted. "Gotta run." He kissed Josie on the cheek. "Carmen Luca, the little weasel, was spotted at the park. I'm gonna bring that woman in today if I have to kill myself."

As he ran out, Josie yelled, "Do not die!"

A glance back at Caleb and she, too, headed for the door.

Improvise, adapt, and overcome. A Marine motto.

"Wait." He jumped to his feet.

She stopped with her hand on the knob. "I just want you to know last night was out of character for me." Her voice was low and quiet. "I don't pick up guys in bars and...you know."

The fact she was still standing here made his day. Now if he could convince her not to leave. "I didn't assume any such thing. I'm a regular at Bad Medicine and I've never seen you. I'm so glad you were there, though. How about a clean slate for both of us?"

She shifted her weight and pivoted, gaze falling on the disaster stacked on the desk. "I've never done admin work before."

Joe emerged from the back. "Thank god you were here for her." He clasped his hands in prayer in front of him and did a slight bow to her. "I thought that gal might hyperventilate and I'd have to call nine-one-one."

Caleb agreed. "Your brother's right – you're a natural with clients. That's the most important part."

She glanced between the brothers. Caleb could see the wheels turning in her head. She was trying to talk herself into staying, or maybe the opposite.

"Josie could handle it if the woman hyperventilated," he reassured Joe, then pointed to his cheek. "I've been on the receiving end of her medical training."

Behind him the fax beeped. Josie scanned the office. "How much does it pay?"

Caleb's anger at Emmanuelle and Carmen and all the rest of them dissipated, her calming presence working its magic. "Fourteen an hour to start. PTO and paid vacation after ninety days. Raises are quarterly with a performance review after six months."

Joe grabbed the papers from the machine and began searching the desk. "It pays whatever you want, if you can start today and find me a pen."

Josie's lips twitched. She retrieved the pen from the clipboard and handed it to him. "Sixteen an hour, with a raise after thirty days. PTO starts accumulating now."

"Done." Joe took it with a smile and they shook.

Josie looked at Caleb again. "Well?"

He motioned toward his office. "I'll draw up paperwork and we'll get you on the payroll."

She shooed him away and sat in the spot he'd vacated. "I'll take care of that. You go do whatever it is you do."

NINE

The desert at night was no place for sissies.

Cooper Harris watched from his lookout spot as Ronni walked the half mile to the drop-off. In his scope, her silhouette was a liquid shadow under the partial new moon, the deep purple of the sky with its normal cascade of stars hid behind errant, drifting clouds.

A coyote howled, then fell deathly silent. A predator's reticence. A moment later, a rabbit's shrill cry cut through the pregnant air. Dinnertime.

In her black clothes, hood on her head, Ronni picked up her pace. He almost missed it, but noticed her shift slightly as her hand went to her gun in its holster.

Cooper hoped the snakes and scorpions knew to take cover. A woman on a mission, his agent was in no mood to give quarter. Nothing would stop her from recovering the information Thomas had left for them.

The temperature was dropping. The overhead cover of clouds thickening. Heat lightning flashed miles away.

Storm moving in.

"I see the boulder." Her voice was hushed as it came through the earpiece. "Looking for the drone now."

Cooper scanned the vicinity, his elbows on the rock under his perch beginning to complain. *Should have brought my guards.* Tomorrow, he'd be sore from forgetting the padded protection. He slowly swept the rifle and scope from west to east. "No party crashers in sight. You're clear."

Another subtle shift as she tugged the gun free and went into a defensive, ready stance. Her approach slowed, wary.

She knew he would keep her safe, but the woman they were after hadn't become an international cartel leader by being stupid or careless. She wasn't their normal drug or gang leader. She was a thief, of all things, but still highly dangerous. If Thomas had taken this level of caution to get information to them from his undercover mission, they needed to recognize the threat was real.

No one, animal, snake, or human was going to take Ronni by surprise. "I see it."

His eyes followed her as she walked the southern area of the giant boulder bigger than a skyscraper. It was one some of the locals claimed had bad juju and avoided. Ancient indigenous people had left their mark on it thousands of years ago, depicting odd stick drawings that resembled aliens and hybrid human and animal shapes.

He heard her breathing become more labored as she skirted outcroppings and smaller rocks. They knew the drone was here, but not the exact location. The GPS on it had malfunctioned before they could home in on it, possibly from smacking into one of the ancient stones, or some other misfortune.

The clouds parted briefly and a drop of moonlight flashed off metal. Cooper zoomed in on it, ready to shout a warning in case it was an ambush, but he grinned when he saw the giant bug near a large opening. "Three meters east. See the break in the stone that looks like a doorway?"

Her feet shifted direction. "Roger that."

A moment later, she hit pay dirt.

He watched as she scanned the immediate area, pocketed the firearm, and began working on the drone. Her nimble fingers opened the compartment and he felt a rush of relief when she said, "Got it."

Excellent. Now they just had to find out what was on the USB Thomas had tucked inside.

Minutes later, Ronni and Cooper hopped inside his truck. As he drove out of the desert, she inserted the drive into a laptop. A sheen of sweat shone on her face in the light of the screen.

Cooper checked his rearview, making sure they hadn't picked up any hitchhikers.

All clear.

His relief was short-lived.

"Oh hell," Ronni said. "This is not good."

Cooper's phone buzzed. Celina. "What is it?" He glanced at her best friend in the passenger seat. "Is he okay?"

Her focus continued to stay on the monitor, gaze darting back and forth as she read. "Better tell Celina you won't be home tonight."

Fuck. He jabbed the speaker button. "Hey, hon."

His wife's voice was always a balm to his heart, but right now, he was about to get an earful, sure as shit. "You promised."

He was not supposed to be on the outskirts of San Diego, hunting down drones in the desert. They were supposed to be celebrating her new promotion. Via, their daughter, was at her grandparents for a sleepover.

Tiny drops of rain began to hit the windshield. "I'm sorry."

Her voice filled the cab. "How many times have I heard that lately?"

Yep, one big-ass storm was moving in, and he was about to be caught square in the center of it. "I'm going to be late, but I will make it up to you."

A fed-up sigh filled the truck. "Ronni? Do you have anything to do with this?"

Ronni glanced up and grimaced silently. Busted. "We just obtained crucial information on a top-priority case," she said. "We have to follow-up."

"I need him for three hours, tops. Surely you and the others can handle whatever emergency this is for that long."

Ronni chewed on her bottom lip. "Yes and no. We can do research and devise a plan, but we may need Coop to call Director Dupé and set some things in motion. Warrants or other elements."

A loaded pause. "Is anyone going to die tonight if you don't?"

Ronni's face was somber, her determination and resolve surfacing again. "Actually, yes, that is a possibility." Her voice dropped several notches and Cooper's stomach along with it. "It's Thomas, Celina. He's in mortal danger."

TEN

T *he next day*

MAYBE SOMEDAY SHE'D get her LPN. She'd go in to physical therapy.

Right now, Josie didn't have two nickels to rub together, and this job was a start.

It wasn't going to be easy working around Caleb all the time, but she'd been in worse situations. If she could ignore his ardent eyes and amazing body, forget about their hour in his extended cab, she could earn some money, keep an eye on Bruno, and dig herself out from under her current situation without her brother having to find out.

The previous day, she'd entered a fake address on her employment form, hoping Caleb wouldn't notice. If anyone said anything, she'd pretend she'd simply made a mistake, and as long as she was taking care of all the filing, who would see it?

Caleb brought her coffee, Joe told her he was available if she had questions, and Malachi – Caleb's twin – seemed relieved she'd come back.

Aboard a sinking ship. From the disaster still on the desk, she was going to need patience and plenty of caffeine, today and every day after. At least her predecessor had set up a decent filing system and it'd only be a matter of time before she'd clear the piles of paperwork.

"There's a three-ring binder with directions and info on the system we use," Caleb said, scanning the tops of the matching file cabinets. "Our last office manager created it."

"Already found it," Josie assured him, and stared at him until he slunk away.

He was correct. Whoever the previous gal had been, she was definitely perfect for this job, the detailed instructions protected in plastic page holders, and each section was labeled and color-coded.

By lunchtime, Josie had created an empty spot in the center of the desktop, had taken several calls and passed messages to the brothers, and met another of the apprehension agents, a guy named Martell Owings.

"Call me Montana," he'd told her. He definitely rocked a cowboy vibe, with a hat, boots, and an oversized belt buckle.

Bruno brought her lunch, and Caleb stayed out of her hair for the most part.

She was going through a backlog of voicemails when a man and woman entered. The guy was taller than Caleb and looked like a linebacker with his broad shoulders and muscled arms. The woman had beautiful mocha colored skin, the tips of her short hair dyed an orangey-red. She was barely as tall as Josie.

It was easy to know people's heights, thanks to the measuring stick someone had glued next to the doorframe. She assumed it was in case those coming and going ever caused trouble. Like bank tellers trained for situations involving robbery and other crimes, it was handy to have.

The camera in the corner might be also.

Josie had already made a mental note to find out if they routinely had troublesome visitors.

"You must be new," the man said. He held a manila envelope in his hands. "Caleb or Malachi around?"

Her ESP didn't go off, but she knew he'd had training—cop or military—from how he carried himself. His companion offered a handshake. "I'm Ronni. This is Cooper. We're with the SCVC Taskforce."

Josie nodded as if she understood what that meant. "Have a seat. I'll get Caleb."

Instead of buzzing him through the phone, she walked to his office. The door was open and she knocked on the wooden frame as she stuck her head in.

A smile broke over his face when he saw her. "How's it going?"

"There are two people here to see you. From some taskforce?"

The smile evaporated. "Harris?"

She shrugged. "Cooper and Ronni."

He stood, tossing a pen on the desktop. "That can't be good."

He followed her to where Cooper stood staring out the front window. The men shook, and Ronni and Caleb acknowledged each other.

"We have a situation." Cooper handed the envelope to Caleb. "We're gonna need your help."

Josie returned to her desk, pretending not to eavesdrop.

He accepted, opening it and pulling out several papers halfway. He scanned the top sheet. "Dover Garnet? Tell me you have a lead on her."

Ronni shook her head. "Afraid not. Not exactly, anyway."

Caleb motioned to the hallway. "Let's go to the meeting room. You guys need coffee?"

Cooper said yes, Ronni declined. Caleb turned to Josie. "Could you tell Malachi and Joe we need to have a meeting?"

"Sure. I'll bring the coffee, too."

He nodded his appreciation. "If you want, you can sit in on this. You might as well learn the ropes about some of our current cases."

"What about the front door?"

"You'll hear the bell if anyone enters."

He disappeared, all business now, and she went to round up the others.

Once she delivered the refreshments and took the last open seat, she placed a yellow notebook on the table and added the day and time. Then she listed those in attendance, and the name of the person they were discussing. It was more for her benefit than anyone else's, and she planned to do nothing more than stay in the background and listen.

"Before we go any farther," Caleb said, "I want to introduce our new office manager, Josie Jackson."

Ronni and Cooper both nodded at her. "You've got a big job," Cooper said, and Josie wondered if he was being sarcastic or serious. His tone suggested he was poking Caleb and his brothers a little, but his features were grave.

Her ESP nudged her, letting her know that was his normal behavior.

"Nice to meet you," Ronni said.

Cooper turned to Caleb. "I know Dover is one of your skips, and we need your help to apprehend her and bring down Ali Karo. She is our ultimate target. Thomas is undercover with her cartel, and he came across information regarding Dover."

"What kind?" Caleb asked.

"Our Hollywood Hacker is working for Karo, and has been exposing corrupt government officials and federal undercover agents. It's been hit and miss, but she's about to release a set of names of DEA and ATF agents to other black-market cartels. Karo's having her auction it off. The highest bidder gets the list."

Joe sat back in his chair and whistled softly under his breath. "Celebrity dirt isn't enough for her these days?"

"We've been searching for her for months," Caleb said. "Is Karo hiding her?"

"Thomas can't find her; he only knows about their plans due to her reaching out to Karo two days ago." Cooper's grave expression didn't change. "He believes Dover is couch surfing at the moment and staying underground as much as possible. The auction is scheduled to go live in three days."

"The message came via an email Thomas intercepted." Ronni worried the band on her left ring finger. "If Karo figures out Thomas is a UC agent, and the names of the others are blown, we have dozens of people in serious trouble. Some are so deeply under, that even finding them or contacting them to warn them, is nearly impossible in this time frame."

Josie sensed how worried Ronni was about Thomas, and her natural radar picked up on the fact they were more than co-workers.

She knew all about the Hollywood Hacker, and wondered if she'd even met her on one of her trips to the Legends Coffee Bar where she'd gone to work on her script. That's where she'd met big time director, Glen Pember, and pitched her idea to him. The bar was a known hangout for scriptwriters and occasionally, directors and producers. She'd even seen celebrities grabbing coffee and discussing potential movie roles with those big wigs.

Cooper tapped the envelope, now lying on the table

between him and Caleb. "Karo typically deals in stolen items, including high-end art, and this seems out of her normal MO, but we think there may be a link between her and Senator Constance Brim."

Malachi lifted his brows. "Has the senator been dabbling in illegal activities?"

Ronni twisted her ring again. "She's suspected of accepting illegal campaign contributions, and we think Karo is possibly one of her funders."

Josie made notes, her hand flying, as ideas came to her. Two powerful women, one a criminal, one a political powerhouse, helping each other out? She put several question marks around that information.

Cooper toyed with the edge of the envelope. "The taskforce is handling the Brim angle, but the list of UC agents cannot go viral. We have to stop Dover, and handcuff Karo."

As the group discussed possibilities and aired their concerns, Josie saw Caleb's deep respect for Cooper and Ronni, along with his concern for this Thomas fellow.

As the meeting wound down, Cooper rose and stretched. "If there's any way you can find where Dover's hiding, we need you to do it. Our computer guy, Bobby, traced that email to a public computer at the San Diego State library. If I had the manpower, I'd haunt that place twenty-four/seven, but I'm trying to keep tabs on Karo and, obviously, my agent. The investigation into Brim has to be done with kid gloves and if I have to pull Thomas, that will blow the whole thing."

"Understood," Caleb said, making a note.

Ronni stood as well. "If we find Dover in the next forty-eight hours and shut her down, we all get what we want. Thomas will be safe to continue, and you'll have the Hollywood Hacker."

Caleb pushed to his feet and stuck out his hand to Cooper. "I will find this woman and bring her in."

ELEVEN

T*wenty-four hours later*

CALEB WAS A DETERMINED MAN, but he still had no good leads on Dover. He'd spent hours the previous afternoon and night digging into her past acquaintances, family, and even her enemies.

He'd been on campus for hours, watching the library closely, the last photo of her in hand. He'd asked around, but no one had seen her, and he suspected she'd changed her appearance enough that she blended with the variety of interesting characters the university housed.

Months ago, he'd reviewed her life in detail when she'd gone on the lam. She was sneaky, for sure, and he despised anyone who could best him.

Dozens of phone calls had led nowhere, and that morning

he'd hit the street, trying to track down all the people he'd talked to in the past. He'd hoped a few might be more loose-lipped now, but it seemed they honestly had no idea where she'd disappeared to.

He was chasing a ghost. No one had seen or heard from her since the last time he'd put out feelers to find her. Since she'd skipped on her hearing in the summer, he'd kicked himself repeatedly for taking the job. He knew better than to provide bail for a hacker – they were high-risk entities, able to change their online identity with ease and create an assortment of fake IDs. Stealing information to keep them a step ahead of him was their forte.

He and Malachi had started Bondsman Brothers after leaving the Marines, and they'd hired veterans who couldn't find decent work in other professions. In general, their business was more than eighty percent closed to the public, a majority of the fugitives they went after directly tied to the government, who rarely wanted it publicized. With their background and training, they had a knack for thinking like their bounties.

In the past year, the biggest case they'd taken had been hunting Samantha, and Joe had been tasked with that. A very risky bounty, since the two had been partners and lovers, but Sam had been framed by her boss at the Agency. All had ended well when she and Joe teamed up to take the woman down.

The rest of the business relied on general bail jumpers and fugitives. Plenty of those around, including today's quarry. Usually, Bruno and Martell handled them, leaving Joe and Caleb to manage the more delicate cases. Malachi was lead dog, always pulling the eldest card. He'd been born a minute sooner and Caleb cursed him for it every day.

"Come on, Dover," he muttered under his breath, keeping his gaze locked on the stream of kids coming in the double doors. He'd settled in a comfy couch just inside the entrance, giving him a clear view and had his cell in hand, pretending to be texting with someone. Tall windows allowed generous light, and he'd done his best to blend in, wearing a mascot sweatshirt and donning a backpack. It was filled with listening and tracking equipment, rather than books, but they gave the thing weight, suggesting he was a student with a full schedule. "Show yourself."

The only good thing about the situation was that tracking her kept his thoughts mostly off Josie. She'd already done wonders in her new position, but things still felt awkward between them. He needed to act like he hadn't seen her naked, and that was asking a lot.

Shutting down his attraction to her was impossible. The best he could do was stay out of the Bondsman Brothers, or lock himself in his office.

Focus.

After another hour, his butt hurt and he decided to take a break. He picked up sandwiches and drove to the office.

When he arrived, Ronni was talking to Josie, and Samantha was there to pick up Joe for lunch.

Josie's face lit up when she saw him and his pulse did a hop. His frustration over Dover's no-show dissolved. "Hey," he said.

'Cuz he was suave like that.

Her smile was so rare, it left him dumbstruck. His mind flashed back to the truck and her lazy, satisfied grin after her third climax.

She held up a photo. "Ronni has a more recent picture of Dover. I made copies and gave them to everyone, and this is for you."

Sure enough, their gal had altered her appearance. "Thanks," he said to both women, trying to focus on the case rather than his suddenly raging hormones. "No luck at the college. She's definitely changing up her routine."

Samantha nodded. "Bobby and I have been haunting some of the online chat rooms where she might hang out, and we've come up with nothing either. She's being really careful."

"She could be anywhere." Ronni heaved a sigh. "I wish Coop would pull Thomas. Karo and Garnet make a wicked team. We still have to stop them to save the identities of the UC agents, but the risk to Thomas, inside Karo's lair, is making me crazy."

Caleb knew Ronni and Thomas were more than coworkers.

"Don't give up yet. One way or another, Caleb will find Dover and bring in Ali, too," Josie insisted. She had an expression on her face suggesting this was fact.

His chest puffed a bit at her confidence in him. "Dover is going to make a mistake, get cocky. The hackers always do."

Ronni nodded, but it was half-hearted. Samantha squeezed her arm.

Joe emerged from his office. "I've cleared my afternoon of meetings," he told Caleb. "I'll hit the streets with you to help search."

"Cool. Go have lunch and we'll regroup later."

Sam and Joe left; Ronni, too, and it was just him and Josie.

All alone in the office.

Which did nothing for his hormones. All they needed to do was lock the door and send the phones directly to voicemail.

"Are you okay?"

He cleared his throat and shifted behind a file cabinet so she wouldn't notice his bulging cock. "Brought you some lunch."

"Awesome!" She accepted the bag and thanked him. "I have a theory on Dover."

He'd already started walking away but this stopped him.

She had that look again...as if she knew something he didn't. His big brain kicked in. "Let's hear it."

"Grab a chair." She motioned for him to pull one up, excitement evident in her features. "And try to keep an open mind, okay?"

TWELVE

J osie studied the picture as Caleb made himself comfortable at her desk. Then, stewing over whether she should even go down this road, she got up and grabbed a couple of sodas from the refrigerator and brought them back.

"Sort of on a time crunch, you know," he said around a bite, his full attention on her. "Spill your theory."

Hard to hide your secrets when the folks involved in them were part of his investigation. "Give me a sec. I'm thinking."

She could feel the frustration rolling off him in waves. He was so determined, so...scared. If he didn't stop Dover, there were a lot of agents who might die, as well as numerous criminals who could get away.

Starving, she dug around in the bag and was happy to see it was takeout from her favorite sandwich joint. Bruno had taken her there the first day she hit town and she hadn't been back in a long, long time.

Withdrawing the food, she spread out the napkin before unwrapping it.

"Josie."

"Huh?" She looked up to see him popping the tab on the soda, continuing his laser stare. Time was up to debate what she was about to do. "Right."

She shuffled through the folder on Dover lying on the desk. "I didn't recognize her from this old picture." She held up the arrest photo that had been added upon intake. "When I saw her, she had longer hair, and it was red."

Caleb stopped drinking and set down the can. "When you saw her where?"

"When I first got back to the States and I was in L.A. I was working on a…project." Better not to tell him what that was. Not even her brother knew about the script and how writing about her experience had saved her from going crazy during the long weeks of surgery and therapy. "I would go to Legends Coffee Bar sometimes, and this guy was there, Glen Pember. He hung out a lot, like many other scriptwriters and Hollywood folks. So did this woman."

She bit into the sandwich. "They sometimes came in almost simultaneously, although they always ignored one another inside. Not sure why, but I assume they didn't want to be seen together. She changed her appearance regularly, but that's not unusual in L.A. On occasion, they left within minutes of each other. Again, a big assumption, but maybe they met up once they cleared the shop."

He continued to stare at her. "Who the hell is Glen Pember?"

This was going to be tough to explain without telling him about her script. About what was currently happening *with* it, because of Glen's betrayal.

"A Hollywood screenwriter and director." Sheer luck had landed her in his orbit. "While you were gone, I did some digging and realized her connection to him could be how she keeps getting dirt on certain celebrities. I mean, how do you think she figured out which to blackmail?"

Caleb continued eating, his lunch nearly gone. "She used this guy's link to them."

"Bingo. I don't have proof, but my gut says that has to be part of it. The Hollywood Hacker is sneaky and has done a good job keeping her true identity, including her face, hidden. Do you know how many different arrest photos are on the internet of her? None of them match. Not only is she an expert in changing her physical appearance, she knows how to hide in plain sight on the World Wide Web, by planting plenty of false information out there. Glen could get her on sets where they were filming, might have shared personal emails and details about various celebrities he was working with. Maybe she hacked their phones and computers while she was there. She might have even bugged their trailers and limos."

He took his last bite, chewing slowly as he considered it. "Why didn't anyone make the connection previously?"

She swallowed and took a quick sip of her soda. "They've been hiding their relationship, and again, because she's so elusive. I just happened to be in the right place at the right time, and noticed their comings and goings, which led me to have a hunch there was something going on between them they didn't want made public."

"An illicit affair. She might have been using Pember without him knowing it."

The sandwich was a Southern Cali Veggie Eggroll—her favorite, with layers of Asian vegetables and a special sauce blend that made her taste buds nearly orgasm. "Affairs are a dime a dozen in Hollywood, and yes, I'd bank on the fact she's been using him for something more than sex. Whether he's in on it or not, hard to say."

He toyed with a pen on the desk. "A covert business arrangement."

"But what was he getting out of it?" she wondered out loud. "Sex? Is that it?"

"When it comes to men, that's usually enough." He watched her, taking a long drink. There was that heat in his eyes that flared every so often between them and made her toes curl.

"Could be power or revenge," she offered, clearing her throat. She tipped the can up for a sip, breaking the intensity of the moment. A stream of liquid went down the wrong pipe, causing her to cough, throat burning.

Caleb handed her an unused napkin. "You okay?"

She wasn't, clearly, but she nodded, dabbing her teary eyes and getting her coughing under control. He got up and brought back a bottle of water.

Around her tight throat, she thanked him and sucked some down, the cool liquid soothing. "Thanks."

He crushed his can before tossing it across the room into a recycle bin. "Are you gonna tell me why you were at this coffee bar hanging out with scriptwriters and directors?"

Nope. When he said it out loud like that, though, it seemed kinda obvious. "I like their coffee. They have a second shop here in San Diego. If you haven't tried their triple espresso, you really should."

For the first time in the past twenty-four hours, Caleb smiled. He crinkled up the wrapper and made a shot at the garbage can. It was a slam dunk. "I need to find this Pember and wring his neck until he gives her up."

She didn't need Caleb to pin down Glen and discover her secret, but she might have to risk it in order to put him on Dover's trail.

It had only been a few days since she'd been on the movie lot and seen Dover in her made-over persona. Not that she'd recognized her then. Josie's mind hadn't been focused on anything other than the fact Glen had stolen her script. Lotta good that had done her. "I may have spotted them recently not far from here. I didn't know who she was until I saw Ronni's photo."

"Was it at the bar?"

She shook her head. "I've got his address – Pember's. You might want to start there and check him out. Tail him, find her if they cross paths. I know time is of the essence, but you should do a stakeout."

He rose from the chair, excitement oozing from him. "Give me that address."

"Use caution." She held up a warning finger. "He could be your best lead, and you don't want to tip him—or her—off. You think she's hiding now? Wait until she discovers you on her trail."

Placing both fists on the desk, he leaned forward, placing his face in front of hers. "Are you schooling me on picking up a skip?"

She put down the portion of uneaten sandwich, steeling her backbone so she didn't lean away. Heat pooled low in her belly as she met his stare head-on. "I'm suggesting caution. I know you're rushed to nab her and stop what's going on with the undercover agents, but..."

"I'm teasing, JJ. You did good." He grinned and the heat shot lower, her body burning with need for him. "Really good, in fact. This is the best news I've had all day. I could kiss you right now."

Her breath caught. Move an inch and he could do just that. Why was it so hot in here? She needed another drink.

Make that a cold shower.

He backed away, threw up both hands, his face morphing

from excitement to worry. "I didn't mean that, like, in the literal sense. The kissing thing. Well, actually I kinda do, but I'm not going to do anything inappropriate. I swear." A hand went to his heart, an oath. "You work for me now, and you're invaluable. I don't want to make things awkward again."

Phew. She didn't want that either.

Except, she kind of did.

At least the kissing part.

Which would lead to more…like his extended cab again.

Cold shower, hell. She needed Siberia at this point.

Flustered, she broke eye contact and took a yellow sticky note from the desk. "Here's his address, and a couple places he hangs out. I'd start by watching his place."

Caleb nodded, back to business, and read it over.

Josie called up all of her determination. "I'm coming with you on the stakeout."

He lifted his gaze to hers and smirked. "Have you ever been on one before?"

She wiped her hands on a napkin, shaking her head. "I have plenty of experience finding people. I won't be any trouble, and I can help you."

Plus, she could keep an eye on any meeting that might arise between Glen and Caleb, and hopefully steer the conversation away from her and her stolen script if need be.

She waited for him to say no, already preparing her next argument.

"Okay."

"I know I'm not a bounty hun…"—she fumbled over her words. "Wait. That's it?"

The way his eyes bore into hers, she knew he sensed she was hiding a lot from him, but he wasn't going to put her on the spot. "Yep."

She appreciated that, and wondered if they might both get what they wanted.

She was going to stop Glen Pember from filming her story, one way or another. And if that meant bringing him down with the Hollywood Hacker, even better.

THIRTEEN

Caleb liked action; stakeouts not so much.

As late afternoon wore into evening, his butt was starting to get numb and he needed to take a piss.

The upside? He was snug in his truck with Josie, pornographic images playing through his mind continuously as he sat mere inches from the spot where he'd made love to her two nights ago.

Sharing space wasn't the hard part, but keeping his hands off her was. They'd already gone through the top ten conversation starters, and she'd grilled him about his childhood. When he inquired about hers, she kept changing the subject.

He'd known Bruno a year or so, neither of them digging into backstories. They talked sports, missions they'd been on, and their work. Now Caleb wished he'd asked more about Bruno's family.

"Why did you take Dover's case?" Josie asked.

She'd donned dark sunglasses and a Padres ball cap. Her hair was long and straight, down around her shoulders instead of the usual ponytail.

Dover had gotten caught for exposing one of the hottest actors in L.A., but Xavier Denning was more than a pretty face.

He was the son of a high-ranking Pentagon official.

The fact Dover had actually been arrested and prosecuted in San Diego had been a bonus for him and his brothers. "Xavier Denning was being investigated by the NSA and Homeland for potential terrorism when she decided to spill about his link to Madam Mary."

"Terrorism?"

The head of an international prostitution ring, specializing in children, Mary was the worst of the worst, in Caleb's opinion. He couldn't fault Dover for outing Denning and a bunch of his buddies, but it had screwed with the FBI's investigation into the man's connections to the 13 Liberation Squad, an Asian terrorist group. "Dover's case was handed to us in order to look into any involvement she might have had with the leakage."

"So it was more than a bounty hunt?"

"Fugitive apprehension. We found no proof she was involved with the terrorist group."

"Wow. That's crazy!"

So far, Glen Pember had not shown up at his ocean side residence. He wasn't directly on the beach north of the city, but he was only a few blocks from the freeway and the smell of ocean air permeated the truck through the open windows. Caleb still had plenty of questions about Josie's connection to the guy, but he was waiting for her to relax. So far, she hadn't.

Her knee bobbed up and down in the passenger seat. "How long were you in the Marines?"

Don't look at her...

Shit, he had to and all bets were off.

There was a bead of perspiration on her neck and he wanted more than anything to wipe it away. Trail his fingers over her skin. Unbutton her shirt and see if moisture was beading on her skin farther down…

She cleared her throat and he raised his gaze. *Busted.* She'd caught him undressing her with his mind.

"Hot, isn't it?" Her voice was husky, soft.

Goddamn. His erection reared and he quickly looked away. He tucked his hand under his leg to keep it from straying. "What was that?"

She fidgeted, toyed with her sunglasses. Maybe she was remembering their night just as he was. "The heat. Intense for this late in the year."

Not what he meant, but… "Brutal summer and now fall."

"You were in the Marines, like my brother, right?"

That was it. She'd asked about his stint. "Long enough, and yet not."

She nodded as if she understood that answer. "B felt the same when he was discharged. A part of him couldn't wait to get home and return to civilian life. Another knew he would never be anything but a Marine."

Maybe she did understand. "And you? Were you ready to get out?"

From the corner of his eye, he saw her shake her head. "It was a shock. I've always been a nurse at heart, helping others. Being the one who needs medical care is odd for me. Since I've been home, things haven't exactly gone well, either. It's good to see Bruno, but other than that? I'd rather be back in the Army."

Yep, he'd been the same off and on since his discharge. He was more of a doer than a delegator like Malachi. "My leave was unexpected. Malachi got hurt, we thought we were gonna lose him, in fact. He was forced out due to his injury, and after that, it wasn't the same for me. We don't have to be together a hundred percent of the time, but something felt wrong once he was no longer in and I was."

She glanced over. "You guys are close, aren't you? Not just because you're twins."

He rubbed a thumb on the steering wheel, glad to have his ride back. "Family is everything. Malachi and I were both damn happy when Joe came to work for us."

The sun was beginning to sink, sending bright orange blades of color across Glen's gated yard. The late fall day was so warm, it was hard to believe the holidays were around the corner. Josie removed the hat and began combing her hair with her fingers. "Bruno and I only have each other, but yeah, it is important. Do your mom and dad live around here?"

"We have dinner with them every week. It's mandatory."

She removed a hair band from her wrist, secured her hair in it, and put the hat back on, pulling the ponytail through the rear opening. "Sounds nice."

An awkward silence fell, their stakeout position off the freeway, the sound of the ocean waves and the car motors going by a constant background noise.

He needed to move, this mindless sitting eating at his nerves. "I'm gonna take a look around. You stay put."

Bailing, he disappeared into a thicket of bushes and finally took a piss. The absolute relief was welcome, and through the cascading flowers hiding him, he noticed Glen liked his toys.

The guy only had a couple of security cameras over his front and back door, and Caleb's reconnaissance showed a stack of surfboards, a kayak, a standup paddle board, and a giant swimming pool in the rear. The garage was a standard two-car, and the house looked far too big for a single guy.

When Caleb returned and hopped into the cab, Josie was tapping away on her cell.

"Good news. Bruno got my car fixed. Not everything, but it's running again."

She wouldn't need his truck anymore.

Damn.

He liked the way it smelled after she'd been in it.

"And just so you know, I've reorganized the caseload, since Bruno wrapped his up an hour ago. I've got everybody listed on the whiteboard with their actives and a column for outstanding paperwork that I need. You have four past due accounts, and I've hired a collection agency to work on those. I also contracted an answering service, so when we're out of the office, we can still get tips and any emergency situations that come up will be directed to me."

"Dare I ask how much that's costing me?"

She shook her head, continuing to work on her phone. "Trust me, I'm watching the budget. In the past thirty days, you've closed out five cases and landed the bounty on three. After the apprehension agent was paid, that left a sum total of a thousand dollars. You had an overdue water bill, which I paid, as well as this month's electric, water, and sewer. The only one outstanding right now is garbage, and I'll handle that tomorrow. What was left covered the answering service and collection agency for the next thirty days. We'll re-evaluate after that and see if the return on investment is worth it before we continue."

Damn. Bruno hadn't been kidding when he said she was organized. He liked that about her, maybe because he was the opposite.

"How's your hip?"

She stopped but didn't look at him. "I'm fine."

"Are you getting disability?"

She hesitated, then went back to typing. "Yes and no."

"What does that mean?

She held up a finger and finished before pocketing the phone. "I'm supposed to be getting it, but my last two checks haven't shown up. The disability office claims they mailed them, but…" She shrugged. "Apparently they're lost in transit."

He adjusted his posture. "I make a call, have one of my friends check on them."

"No." A flicker of fear crossed her features. "I can do it."

At his scowl, she forced a smile, but he could tell it wasn't natural. "Thank you. I appreciate the offer, but really, it's no big deal."

Caleb made a mental note to contact his guy at the VA office anyway. No wonder she was down on her luck. If they hadn't showed up for two months, how was she paying her bills?

"How did it happen?" he inquired.

She put her elbow on the window and leaned on it, rubbing her face. "Bad timing is all. I was flying in to rescue a couple injured soldiers, and we were ambushed."

"Flying?"

She thumbed her chest. "Helicopter pilot."

"Damn, that's hot."

A scathing look cast his way. At least, that's what he assumed she was going for, but honestly, it just made her even sexier. "I took shrapnel in my back and leg, they blew up the helo, several guys didn't make. I did."

His guts crawled. She'd nearly died. And he knew the survivor's guilt on her face intimately.

The old rage flickered in his belly. He'd watched his buddies die, nearly lost Malachi. Death needed to suck it.

"I was stranded for a couple weeks," she continued, "and it's surprising I didn't die too. I'm still not sure why I made it and they didn't. One of the locals patched me up, but I had to keep moving and get to the embassy. It was a long two weeks."

"Holy fuck." Injured and alone. "Behind enemy lines?"

She nodded but went tight-lipped on him. He stewed, his gut telling him there was more to the story. He wanted to push her on it, but he'd learned that didn't work. She was as stubborn as the day was long.

A lot like him.

For a second, he considered the idea he'd met his match.

Needing to do something, he pulled several energy bars from the glove compartment and handed her one. They sat in silence, mindlessly eating as memories of their enlisted time hovered in the air like fog. Watching Glen's house, he couldn't stop fidgeting, feeling like the stakeout was a waste of time.

But having Josie there, even a silent version of her, calmed his need to do something. Soon the sun was setting, darkness enveloping them.

They were getting down to the wire and lives were on the line.

Fucking death.

He would not let Thomas, or anyone else, die on his watch.

A sliver of a waxing moon rose, sending pale light into the cab. Josie sank in her seat and closed her eyes.

It wasn't long before her soft snores filled the space, rising and falling like the waves in the distance.

Caleb watched her, growing sleepy himself, and tried to do little things to keep conscious without waking her. Didn't work.

Just a nap, he told himself. *Fifteen minutes tops.*

He set an alarm on his phone and dozed off.

When he stirred sometime later—the alarm failed to bring him out of his slumber—he found Josie still asleep.

With her head in his lap.

Her hat was on the floor, her hair mussed. Those perfect full lips were parted slightly.

And aww shit, that porn movie started all over again in his head.

Fantasies about her and what he still wanted to do to her filled his mind.

Her breathing was light and easy, and he found himself struggling not to stroke her hair, trace her jawline. The air had cooled considerably and he wished he had a blanket to throw over her, but he was too scared to move and reach for the one in the back.

He stayed put.

Call it. Pull the plug.

Pember hadn't showed and this stakeout was a dead end.

Instead, he sat and watched Josie resting peacefully.

She needed it. Needed a break.

He hoped she dreamed about something fun. That she didn't have nightmares like he did.

Soon sleep came calling for him, and Caleb drifted off, Josie still safe in his lap.

FOURTEEN

Josie came to groggily, a kink in her neck. She yawned and turned to her side, wondering what was jabbing her in the arm. Her pillow seemed firmer than usual, too, and she blinked, frowning when she saw blue jeans, the column of a steering wheel, and an unfamiliar console.

Oh shit. She jerked up, head swimming. Caleb stared out the window, eyes shuttered and hands raised in the air. "I fell asleep, and when I woke up, you were"—he cleared his throat—"in that position. Nothing happened, I swear."

Limp strands of hair fell into her face as she glanced at his lap. Heat crawled up her neck and into her cheeks. "Jeez."

He obviously had a ginormous morning erection, and no doubt having her head there had contributed to it.

Embarrassment singeing her face, she tried to ignore that bulge, and shifted to straighten her shirt and jacket. "Sorry. I, uh..."

Brilliant, Josie. Real smooth.

How exactly did you apologize for falling asleep in your boss's crotch?

Pretty sure the manners experts never included such a predicament in their blogs or books.

Man, she needed to pee. Resettling herself in the passenger seat, she clung to the door and leaned as far against it as possible. "Did Pember ever show?"

Caleb started the truck. "Not that I saw."

Damn it. They were almost out of time. "He's on location. Maybe he spent the night there. Sometimes they do. I should've checked that first."

Caleb put the truck in gear. "You seem to know a lot about this guy."

The sun was coming up, birds singing. The air was cool, but she still felt overheated. "I need coffee, sugar, and a bathroom. ASAP. How about you drop me at the office? Bruno left my car for me. I can run home quick and clean up."

He maneuvered out of the residential neighborhood and headed for the freeway. "Sure." His gaze never quite met hers, apparently continuing the total gentleman act. "You know, you should take the day off. Get some decent rest. You didn't have to stay with me. It's only fair."

Her mouth was dry and her stomach rumbled. "Don't worry, I was on the clock. Don't think you're gonna renege on my paycheck either."

He shot her a glance and a hint of a grin moved his lips. "Oh, I see how it is. Do you want me to drive you home? I can wait while you get ready, if you still want to come in today."

The thought of him watching her shower flashed through her mind and she felt herself turn three more shades of red. "No," she answered too quickly.

He gave her another look, this one full of consternation.

Deep breath. *Smile.* The last thing she needed was for him

to find out about her squatting in the abandoned hangar. "I can just clean up at the office. Save time."

Returning his focus to the road, he said nothing, but the light moment faded. She had the feeling he was mulling over her resistance, and as smart as he was, that might tip him off.

"Why don't we get breakfast?" He passed a slow-moving vehicle. "My treat. We can strategize about where to find Pember, and then figure out showers and fresh clothes from there."

It wasn't ideal, but maybe if she ate and had caffeine, she could get her brain online. Waking up like that had her all messed up. Her joints ached, but all she could think about was this crazy attraction she had to him. "Do you know any place close that has strong coffee?"

He smiled. "Strong or good?"

"Are the two mutually exclusive?"

He made a right turn, merging into a fresh wave of morning traffic. "Not necessarily, if you're willing to go a few extra miles. I know a mom and pop diner not far from here that has the best breakfast you can ask for. The coffee's always hot, strong, and better than what we have at the office."

"Sounds like heaven."

Caleb couldn't believe she'd said yes. She had lots of secrets, and he wondered about where she was living most of all.

The other good thing about Haskell's Diner was the fact they were fast. It wasn't long before he was watching Josie inhale a super-sized breakfast of eggs, sausage, toast, and hash browns.

He'd ordered the same, and was happy to fill his face while observing her. She was still tense, and he didn't know if it was because of what had happened earlier or due to things she was concealing.

She talked a lot when she was nervous, and she brought up several ideas for organizing the office, and he just kept nodding and shoveling food into his mouth.

She's a hurricane. A tsunami when it came to orderliness and structure. It was exactly the kind of thing that should've scared him. Instead, he felt like he should run head first into her.

That did scare him. He didn't do long-term relationships, hadn't even thought about a steady girlfriend in years.

When she was done, she pushed her plate aside, a single triangle of toast in one corner. "That was delicious."

"Thought you might like it. Hopefully all that salt and grease will help us figure out how to catch Dover today."

"I'm hitting the restroom. Let's get coffee to go. We can clean up and hunt down Glen."

He hailed the waitress as Josie left the booth. While he waited for the two drinks, he called Danny about the disability checks. "Our new office manager says she hasn't gotten any in two months," he told his friend. "Check on them, will you? Probably lost in the mail, but she needs that money."

Danny owed him big time and assured Caleb he would follow-up and get back to him as soon as he could.

"Thanks, man."

Annoyance ate at him. The story she'd told him swirled in his mind. Someone who should be considered a hero was struggling to make ends meet.

Josie came out, face washed and hair combed. The coffees were delivered and Josie picked up both as Caleb paid and they took off for the office.

THE MOMENT they walked in the door, Caleb was assailed by Martel. "Bagged another. Need my cut." He glanced at Josie, beaming with pride. "Mark it off your board, JJ. Montana Owings always gets his man. Or woman," he added with a wink.

"Can it wait?" Caleb said. "We're running down Dover Garnet and we're on a deadline."

"Dude, my tenth wedding anniversary is tomorrow. Gotta buy the wifey a nice gift, you dig?"

Caleb grimaced. "Fine. Come on back and I'll cut a check."

The two disappeared down the hall. Josie grabbed her car keys from where Bruno had left them on the desk. She scribbled a note to Caleb about feeding her cat, and hurried out.

Her vehicle still sounded like it was on its last leg—or tire in this case. She'd told Bruno she'd reimburse him as soon as she could, and he'd told her not to worry about it.

But she did.

Bruno was her hero, inside and out. He'd been taking care of her since their mother died when Josie was only thirteen.

Bruno had been fifteen.

Their dad had left years before.

Child services had come calling, but Bruno was too cunning to let that break them up. He had friends and he knew how to dodge the overworked case workers and find them a place to stay, week after week, night after night.

Eventually, he'd convinced one of their distant cousins to take them in, going to work in the man's auto body shop for room and board. Josie had spent every afternoon after school learning about cars from him.

The plane hangar came into view and she parked in her favorite hiding place. Keeping a low profile was second nature and it felt a little like home here.

After feeding her cats, who cried at her for being late, she showered quickly and dressed. Admitting she was actually excited to get back and keep working on this case surprised her. Organizing the chaos had brought a sense of satisfaction to her that she hadn't had in a long time.

Being on the hunt for Glen and Dover made the blood race in her veins.

Being around Caleb had a similar effect.

For different reasons, obviously, but it was good to feel alive again.

She placed a couple calls before getting back in her ride. Whether or not Glen had stayed on the set overnight wasn't important. Her research confirmed he'd returned to work that morning, filming her story.

Fresh anger soared through her, her mind going over various options as she drove. She wanted to tell Caleb the truth, but she needed to figure this out on her own. She needed an attorney who specialized in intellectual property, and she couldn't get that until she had a significant deposit. Another week, and she'd get her first pay, and then she'd go after the bastard.

It would probably mean forgoing rent on a decent place for a while. She'd also have to put off repaying Bruno for the repairs. But she could keep on taking care of the stray cats, at least, and the hangar wasn't so bad. The Navy had only abandoned it recently, and it still had power and plumbing. No telling how long before the paperwork finally got through and those amenities went bye-bye, but she figured the government owed her. For now, she'd use the measly amount of electricity and water necessary without an ounce of guilt.

Glen was the only real lead they had at the moment to find Dover. She bit her bottom lip. Somehow, she had to ditch Caleb and check out the set, this time with a new target.

Part of her urged to go there now. She could call him, tell him she came down with a headache or stomach issue. He'd already encouraged her to stay home, so maybe she could tell him she'd changed her mind and was taking him up on his offer.

But if she spotted Dover and alerted Caleb, her lie would be blown.

Lies were like the proverbial house of cards. Once one crumbled, she feared the rest might, too.

Better to stick with Caleb, find Dover, and potentially ruin Glen's career in the process.

Because if he was assisting Dover in her enterprises, he was also going down.

Josie turned on the radio and sang at the top of her lungs. One way or the other, she was going to put him out of business.

And make sure he didn't film that movie.

Pulling into the parking lot at Bondsman Brothers Agency, she was surprised to see Malachi and Joe leaning over the open hood of Malachi's SUV.

She parked under the lone palm tree, locked up, and called, "What's up?"

When Malachi explained the symptoms, she frowned. "Let me have a look."

The two backed away, Malachi wiping grease-stained hands on a towel. She checked and cross-checked all the obvious items—spark plugs, battery connections, oil gauge. Nothing was amiss.

Inside the cab, she turned the key and listened.

That wasn't a good sound.

She'd heard it before. Different type of vehicle, but her intuition told her she was spot on.

Cutting the engine, she climbed out. "You have sand in your gas tank."

The brothers glanced at each other as though she were speaking a foreign language. "How would sand get in my gas tank?" Malachi asked.

"Were you joy riding in the desert?"

Joe snickered. "Malachi doesn't joy ride."

Malachi hit him with the rag. "I like a clean vehicle. She's my baby. I take care of her."

She shrugged. "If we were in Afghanistan, I'd say Mother Nature did it. Here?" The street and buildings glowed in the late morning sun. "Someone must have intentionally put it in there."

He groaned and smacked a hand against the side. "Are you kidding me?"

Joe started laughing, softly at first then louder. "I bet it was Goodwin. Revenge by sand."

She assumed it was an inside joke since Malachi seemed to give that theory credit and began swearing about the "no-good SOB."

"How did you know?" Joe asked as he accompanied her into the office, leaving his brother to tend to the SUV.

"Cars, helicopters, human bodies – they're all systems, and if you understand how they work, how they sound and move when they're healthy, it's relatively simple to figure out what needs fixing. Sometimes all you can do is simply listen and let it tell you what's wrong." She shrugged. "I worked on various ones in the Army, and I've heard that kind of noise in the desert before."

She was carrying the coffee cup from the diner as she went through the back door, and nearly ended up wearing the last dregs of it when Caleb crashed in to her on his way out.

It was like hitting a wall.

As she ricocheted against the doorframe, he automatically reached to steady her. "Sorry. You okay?"

Joe also put a hand out. "Jeez, Caleb, watch where you're going."

"I got this," was his brother's response. "You following up with Coop on our progress?"

"You mean, lack of?" But Joe took the hint and walked away. "Calling him right now."

Left alone, Caleb returned his attention fully to her. "You disappeared on me."

"I left a note." She wiped at coffee drips on her shirt. "Didn't you see it?"

His level gaze locked on hers. "You must really love that cat."

She moved aside to let the door close. "There are several, in fact. Strays, but still. They depend on me for food and water."

He studied her face, searching for the truth. It made her sweat, but she kept her breathing steady, her return gaze direct.

"I found out where Pember is filming. Thought I'd drive over. I'm gonna search this bastard's car, his trailer, the set... Anything he's associated with to see if I can get a lead on Dover."

Oh boy. There was no keeping him from the movie set, she could only hope he didn't manage to put two and two together.

"I'll go with you," she volunteered, possibly a little too cheerfully. "I can flash Dover's picture around, see if anyone's seen her without tipping off Glen."

It wasn't that she wanted to be spotted by Pember – far from it – but if she could get on the set with Caleb, she might be able to do a little personal investigation herself.

Joe came up behind them. "Coop is out. Left a voicemail. What do you want me on?"

"Stake out. Watch Pember's place for me." Caleb started hitting buttons on his phone. "Sending you the address now. This bastard isn't going to outsmart me again. We're covering all his hangouts. I already put Bruno on the coffee shop."

Joe saluted and walked out.

"The only thing is," she told Caleb as he slipped his cell in his back pocket, "we need to be very discreet. We need to blend in, so no one figures out that we're not part of the film crew."

He shrugged, flipping his palms up. "How do we do that?"

Josie grinned. "We need disguises."

SIXTEEN

O n location, tents and motorhomes, trucks with equipment, and tons of people milling around created a sort of chaos Caleb embraced. At least he had something to go on now. He was gonna track down Dover, and find out exactly why Josie knew so much about Glen Pember.

This set was halfway between San Diego and Carlsbad, but filled with fake buildings as well as fake people. He and Josie were wearing hats, sunglasses, and casual clothes like the majority of those running around. Security was minimal, and it took Caleb all of two minutes to lift ID badges from a vacant chair not far from the entrance.

The sun beat down on them as he handed one to her. She looked at the picture and name and gave him a sardonic brow lift. "Apparently, I've had a sex change and I'm now Fred Willet."

Caleb checked his and realized he at least could pretend to be the guy in the picture, only fifty pounds lighter, bald, and suffering from acne scars on his cheeks. "Stan," he said throwing the lanyard on. "Nice to meet ya."

Josie took off her cap, dropped hers around her neck, making sure it was backwards. Returning the hat to her head, and wiping sweat from her brow, she glanced around. "It's a big lot. Should we split up?"

No way he was letting her out of his sight. "We stick together. We work as a team."

"We're running out of time, though."

He started walking, heading north. Two employees eyed him and Josie, but all they did was nod. "I always hate that in movies when people separate under the weak guise of time constraints or they have a big area to cover. Then, of course, one or more ends up running into the bad guy and getting themselves in trouble."

She fell into step beside him. "Too stupid to live, right? We need to find some of the on-set key grips and lighting people. They'll have been here every day, and should be able to tell us if they've seen Dover in her disguise."

"Good idea. We can also find Pember's trailer and search it."

"Could be tricky getting in and out of that without being spotted."

"Leave that to me." He chuckled quietly. "I'm an expert at camouflage."

She gave him a disbelieving glance. "Sneaking around undercover doesn't seem like a skill you would have."

He feigned mock surprise. "Are you kidding? I'm a ninja when it comes to this shit."

This made her laugh, and the sound did something to him. He wished she'd do it more.

He took out his phone and brought up the picture of Dover. As they passed a short gal with glasses and a clipboard in hand, he stopped her with a smile. "Say, have you seen this woman?"

"She's an extra," Josie added.

The gal barely dipped her gaze, then started walking again. "Nope."

Caleb felt a flare of irritation. He and Josie continued and he muttered, "She didn't even look at it."

They stopped three more people as they made their way around the outskirts of the set. No one admitted to seeing their criminal. He wondered if they should start showing the older photo as well.

They were near a set of trailers, and Caleb was ready to regroup, when a young guy in shorts and a tank top passed by and waved at Josie, as if he knew her. "Hey, how you doing?"

Josie waved back. "Good, you?"

Before the kid could get far, she turned on the charm and made her way over to him, grabbing his arm. "I really could use some help if you have a minute. I've got to find this woman" – she held up her phone with the same picture displayed – "but she's nowhere around. Have you seen her?"

The guy studied Josie, offering her a flirty smile. "You must be new. I'm Tyler."

Josie put on a matching smile and cocked her hip. "I am, actually, and that's why I gotta find her before I get in trouble. Glen told me she was here, but I haven't seen her."

Tyler glanced at it and Caleb saw recognition dawn on his face. He studied it a little closer. "I saw someone who looked like her leaving Glen's trailer about twenty minutes ago."

A rush of exhilaration ran through Caleb's veins.

"Is Glen here?" Josie questioned.

"He's out in the desert today. The enemy attack scene."

Josie's face changed. "Oh really? You mean where the heroine is injured?"

His curiosity piqued once more. Josie seemed to know an awful lot about Glen and this movie.

Tyler nodded. "The studio wants the hero to rescue Latoya. Makes a better love story."

Josie's brows dipped. "Latoya?" Then she seemed to understand. "Oh hell, you've got to be kidding. They changed my na..."

She cut off, both men looking at her. A fresh smile replaced the frown and she took a step back. "Thanks for the help. Where's Glen's trailer again?"

Suspicion crossed Tyler's face. "I thought you two were part of the crew." He eyed their stolen badges.

Caleb moved forward, grabbing Josie by the elbow. "We are," he covered smoothly. "We haven't read the final script, though. We only started yesterday."

He hustled Josie away, and she waved to Tyler over her shoulder. Pulling her close to his side, Caleb lowered his voice. "You're going to tell me what's going on, right?"

She scanned the area. "Why would Dover be here if Glen's out in the desert?"

"Maybe she knew he'd be gone, and she came for something."

Josie shook her head. "She's living in his place, I'd bet money on it."

"We've raised suspicion, so we better finish this quick. I wanna find that trailer."

They found a row of them, and tried to look inconspicuous as they searched for Glen's. "There." Josie pointed, and sure enough, one of the fanciest they'd seen had a big sign on the side door with Pember's name and Director underneath it.

"Okay," Caleb said, "here's what we're gonna do."

Suddenly, Josie's body went rigid. She grabbed his wrist with one hand, pointing with the other. "Caleb, there she is!"

Following her gesture, he saw a tall woman in camo, a long coat, and a dark hat ten yards away. The giant tote over her shoulder was the same in the latest pic they had of her.

His feet were moving before his brain, and he broke into an all-out run.

Dover Garnet was walking out the main gate.

SEVENTEEN

They raced after her.

"Hey!" Caleb called, trying to catch her attention.

He was faster, and Josie silently cursed her bad hip.

Caleb stopped, a good ten feet from her, and glanced over his shoulder. He must've seen the pain on her face because he hustled to her, positioning one of her arms around his waist. "Hang on to me."

She hated it, needing him. Needing anyone. "No, go without me. You can catch her."

They weren't even halfway to Caleb's truck, and Dover had already jumped in a tiny blue car and was speeding out of the parking area, sand flying.

"I'm not leaving you. I got the make and model. We'll track her down."

"What if it's stolen?" Josie still felt like shit, her back suddenly screaming in pain, and guilt at causing Caleb to lose Dover crashing through her.

He didn't answer and she knew he was thinking the same thing—and they'd just lost the target.

By the time they got in and pulled out, Dover was long gone. Heading west, the desert sand giving way to hills, Caleb slammed a hand into the steering wheel, his frustration showing. "We have no idea where she's heading."

Pain throbbed up and down her leg, causing her to bite her bottom lip. She'd been pushing too hard, trying to ignore the stiffness and ache from sleeping in the cab, and walking around the set had triggered the injury to flare up. Running after Dover had been a huge no-no.

Exhaustion swamped her, some due to the heaviness of the discomfort, but mostly because she'd screwed up. She rifled through her purse, searching for her meds. She never took any unless it was this bad, and even then, she just rode it out at times. But right now, she couldn't—wouldn't—let her disability stop her from helping Caleb. She had to admit she needed relief.

As they drove, Caleb used his Bluetooth to call Cooper, Bruno, his brothers, and a few others. He put out his own form of an all-points bulletin, alerting as many as he could to their Dover sighting.

"You didn't catch her?" Cooper asked, exasperated.

Josie stared at the bottle of pills, not seeing them. They'd been so close!

"She was too far from us," Caleb answered. "The good thing is we know she's still in the area. She hasn't fled the country. We'll get her."

Josie stared out the window, watching the palm trees and other cars fly by, mentally wishing just one damn thing could go right. She was jinxed, cursed, or had some freakin' nightmare karma hanging over her head.

Squeezing the bottle, she let the pain course through her, made herself feel it. She gritted her teeth, clamping down on the anger inside her.

After finishing his calls, Caleb took the ramp heading southwest, skirting the regional park that stretched for miles. She sat, silent and brooding, until he reached over and grabbed her hand. "Quit beating yourself up. We're going to find her."

"You should've left me."

"Bullshit. Hey." He tugged on her fingers until she glanced at him. "I don't leave anybody behind, no matter what."

The strength of his grip and the confidence in his voice pushed some of the pain away. She held the bottle in her other hand, still debating internally with herself. A part of her wanted to pull away from him and his no-man-left behind motto and continue to brood. It's what she excelled at.

But that wasn't going to do either of them any good. Besides, she'd been through worse than this. She'd survived then, and she was going to get her life back, come hell or worthless humans like Dover and Glen.

She squeezed him. "Thank you."

He nodded, his scrutiny on the road. "I assume those are pain meds. Take them."

He released her, handing her the cold coffee. She accepted it and downed the pills.

They drove around, watching for the blue car. Plenty of similar vehicles, but none the one they wanted.

Caleb asked questions about Glen and the movie, and Josie played dodgeball with most of them. He was putting her on the spot, when a call came in, interrupting his interrogation.

"Yo, Paulie. You got something?"

Paulie, the bartender?

"My bro, Carlos, was speed trapping tourists on I-125.

Might've spotted her taking the turnoff for the college out that way. Grossman, I think it is."

"Thanks, buddy."

He disconnected and punched the steering wheel again. "Dammit, she went north. Should've known."

"So turn around. Maybe she's headed to that college library."

He called Joe instead. "Got a possible sighting." He reeled off the info. "Check it out. I'll meet you as soon as I can."

Then he turned to her. "You're done for today. You need rest and to get off that hip. I'll drop you at your place, then meet up with the others."

"You will not. I'm going with you."

"It's either there or the office. You're off foot duty for now."

"I took my pain meds, I'll be fine."

"Josie." His hands tightened on the wheel. "You're not fucking fine."

"Don't tell me what I can and can't do."

He left the road and turned into a parking lot. "You work for me. I hate to pull the boss card, but I wouldn't allow the others to hunt down a perp in your condition, and I won't let you either. This is dangerous stuff, and I can't watch out for you while I'm chasing a fugitive."

She started to argue, then snapped her mouth shut. She was slowing him down and the lives of undercover agents were on the line. It was time to pull the plug on her stubbornness.

"You're right." She hiked her purse strap onto her shoulder and grabbed the door handle. "I'll get a cab."

A strong hand landed on her arm before she could get out. "The guys are on their way to the college and they'll have Coop's team going as well. I can take you home."

Damn. "Really, it's okay. I can get a ride. My place isn't far from here."

"You're about to drop from pain and exhaustion. Tell me where you live."

Cripes. Now she had to fabricate another lie.

She'd have to have him drop her a few blocks from the base, pretending she lived in one of the suburban blocks of houses nearby. It would kill her to walk all the way to the hangar, but she'd just have to do it. "I'm sorry I couldn't be more help."

He made a noise in the back of his throat. "Are you kidding me? You're the only reason I was able to find her in the first place."

She told him the name of the development near the base and directed him toward it.

A row of houses in a cul-de-sac came into view, and she said that she rented the one on the end. She hadn't expected that he would want to walk her to the door, and when he started to do just that, she put out a hand to stop him. "Get going. I'm fine. I'll get a ride from Bruno to the office after I rest."

He reached over and ran a hand across her chin. "Just stay home and take care of yourself. I've got this under control."

For a moment, she wondered if he was going to kiss her. She also debated whether she was going to let him.

Who was she kidding? Of course she was. His focus dropped to her lips, and she held steady, ready, aching, needing him...

Buzzbuzzbuzz. His phone. He dropped his hand.

She grabbed her purse and opened the door. "Go get her."

As he was backing out of the drive, she prayed no one was home. She waved as he drove away, turning to act like she was going to enter.

When he disappeared from sight, she began the hike through the residential park, swearing with every step. Her leg dragged and she gritted her teeth through the tears that began to bubble up. She wished for her cane, and wasn't that a sorry turn of events.

Dashing them away, she crossed through the open soccer yard, several people on the outdoor track watching her. What should've taken her five minutes, stretched to ten, more. Sweat ran down the back of her neck.

At one point, she had to sit on a bench and rest. A couple stretches and digging deep for determination, she stood a few minutes later, and began the next part of her trek.

By the time she reached the edge of the asphalt and crawled through the open section of gate that had been removed, she was nearly in tears again. Standing still to catch her breath, she rubbed her hip muscle.

Needing something to take her mind off the pain, she focused on seeing the cats, feeding them, washing off in the showers inside the locker room. What she wouldn't give for a sauna right now. Hell, for a beer.

It took another long, agonizing few minutes before she arrived at the hangar. She entered the side door, greeted by meows and furry bodies.

Her whole body ached now, her left hip burning from trying to take the weight from her right, and her breathing was shallow from keeping her upper half tense. She lay down on the cool cement floor and let the cats climb over her, lick her face, nudge her hands.

How long she lay there, she wasn't sure. She fell in and out of sleep for a while, the pain meds beginning to kick in.

It wasn't enough. Not nearly. She would need a muscle relaxant, too, and those things rendered her unconscious for hours. The times she broke down and took one, she cut it in half. Still, it would knock her completely out.

A deep, dreamless sleep would be good, but she had to get back to work. Figure out a way to help Caleb and the others.

When the worst eased, she forced herself from the floor and into the small kitchenette. She fed the cats, petting their soft fur before she trudged slowly to the locker room and stripped.

In the shower, she turned the water as hot as she could stand it and stood under it until it ran cold. Then she went to the locker that held some of her clothes and pulled on a fresh t-shirt and underwear. She was about to head to the cot in the office, when she thought she heard something fall.

Probably one of the cats knocking an item over. They were continually jumping on high surfaces and sending the few remaining items to the floor in various areas.

Rubbing her hair with a towel, she left the room, her mind on the long nap she was going to take. She would wait until tonight for the muscle relaxant, and pray a little rest and the pain meds would help her enough in the next hour or two that she could go in.

The cement floor was cool under her feet as she made her way forward, two of the cats following. As she turned the corner, she dropped the towel. The door was open, and she knew she'd closed it when she'd left yesterday.

As she inched closer, both felines fled. She cocked her head and listened, but heard nothing from inside.

Maybe I didn't get it latched well. One of the cats probably barged in.

She was a foot from the open doorway when pain exploded in the back of her head and she fell to her knees.

More came across her shoulder blades, and she toppled face down, hands flying out to stop the fall.

"You need to find a new job," a woman's voice said as a pair of boots came into view.

Josie's vision was unfocused, blurry. She saw the end of a bat tap against the stranger's legs. They were covered in camouflage pants, the hems tucked into motorcycle boots.

The wood made a soft *thud* sound when it smacked the leather. "Back off of this case, bitch, or you're going to end up dead."

Josie blinked, pushing herself onto her good hip to try and look up, but the next thing she knew, the bat swung again, and everything went dark.

EIGHTEEN

"Josie!" His voice rang out in the hangar, echoing back to him.

This damn woman. Why the hell was she here?

He'd had no luck tracking the blue car, and when he'd backtracked to the house Josie had claimed was hers, he'd found an elderly couple who were quite confused about his request to speak to Josie.

The man mentioned that he'd seen a woman matching her description in the driveway, but she'd taken off for the park.

Caleb had ventured to the outdoor spot, but had seen no evidence of her. When he'd asked a few of the people utilizing the track and basketball hoops, one had pointed him in the vicinity of the empty airplane hangar of the abandoned military base a few blocks over. They claimed she'd gone that way, and another had seen her climb through a hole in the fence.

The place was recently closed, but there were still plenty of offices filled with furniture. He'd been greeted by a variety of feral looking cats. Their curiosity had not won out over the fear and they'd scattered in all directions.

Why was she feeding stray cats here?

Echoing down the hallway, he thought he heard footsteps and shouted again, but no answer came back. He jogged toward where the sounds came from, weaving through several areas and past open glass windows that showed him the airfield.

"Josie," he called once more. "Are you in here?"

He was beginning to doubt himself. Her secrets ran deeper than any he could imagine, and nothing about this matched up with the woman he'd come to know the last few days.

He heard a door bang and he turned left rather than right, the space before him dark and smelling of old metal. There were no windows here, only concrete block walls, a large meeting room...and a great big blob on the floor.

Even though he couldn't make out details, he knew in an instant it was human. "Holy shit."

Sure enough, as he drew closer and fell to his knees beside her, his worst fears were confirmed. Josie was dressed in a pair of underwear and a t-shirt, body limp.

He shook her by the shoulders, saying her name. Then he checked for a pulse.

The steady thrum of it under his fingers reassured him she was still alive, and he blew out a solid breath of relief. But as he shifted her onto her back, he saw a large welt coming up on her left temple.

The room visible past the doorway was dark, but he lifted her into his arms and carried her inside. He tried flicking the light switch but got no response. As he stumbled forward, his hip connected with a desk, and then he saw a cot with a light-colored blanket as his vision adjusted to the shadows.

He made it over to the bed and laid her down, pulling out his phone and turning on the flashlight app. He scanned her with the beam, but could only see the injury to her forehead, her scant clothing giving him an excellent view of everything else.

It appeared there were no other cuts or bruises but he did notice a scar residing above her right hip close to her spine. He straightened her out once more, and she moaned softly.

Setting the phone on the cot next to her, he squeezed her hand, then gently patted her face. "Josie? Come on, woman. Wake up."

She twisted away from his touch, but the action must have created a wave of pain. She grimaced and groaned again. "What...happened?"

"Was kinda hoping you could tell me that."

She blinked, squinting up at him. "Caleb?"

The flashlight beam was enough to see her face clearly. Still, he lowered his to look her in the eyes more carefully and check her pupils. "Yeah, it's me. What the hell are you doing here?"

She lifted a hand, flinching as her fingers touched the bump. "Oh shit."

"Oh shit is right. Josie, you have to come clean with me, and tell me what the hell is going on with you."

She insisted on sitting up, and he held onto her as she swayed from the action. Elbows on knees, she sunk her head into her hands. "My run of bad luck extended to losing my apartment after I couldn't pay rent two months in a row."

He processed that and swore under his breath. "Because your checks didn't come through? Why didn't you tell me? Why didn't you tell Bruno?"

She heaved a tired sigh. "I thought I could get everything straightened out. I didn't want to worry him, and... Honestly, I don't know you well enough to tell my darkest secrets to."

He eased down to sit next to her, rubbing a hand through

his hair. "Seriously? You think I'd judge you after all we've been through?"

"You want to pony up why you're so angry all the time that you pick fights at the bar?"

She had him there. He didn't talk about his shit with anyone. Not even his brothers.

"Thought so." Gingerly, she lifted her head to glance at him. "I'm a hot mess. I didn't exactly want to lead with that, especially after I found out you were going to be my boss."

He teasingly pinched her leg. "I sort of like hot messes."

She sat in silence for a moment. "I struggle with depending on anyone, in case you haven't figured that out. I learned young not to. Bruno is my rock, but he's already done far and away enough for me since we were kids. My independence gets me in some deep holes at times, but I've never been this screwed up before. I'm doing my best, and I *will* get things figured out. I'm not looking for handouts."

He admired her for that, but her stubbornness was even worse than his own. "What happened before I got here?"

She stared toward the desk, but her gaze was a million miles away. He noticed a cane lying on top of it. "It took me awhile to make it here because my hip is so uncooperative. Trekking around on the movie set irritated it, and then trying to walk the several blocks to get here was torture. I managed to feed the cats and take a shower, and I thought I heard something. Assumed it was one of them messing around, but when I got here" – she lifted a hand to motion at the office – "the door was open. I always close it when I'm not here because I don't want the cats to wreck my stuff. I keep food in here. They're rebellious little critters, and they would find it in no time, which would leave me without any. I literally have six protein bars to my name, along with a bag of chips. Until I get paid, I can't afford groceries."

He pointed to a bag of cat food on a high shelf. "So you're feeding them instead?"

"I had a coupon," she said straight-faced.

Feeding strays instead of buying her own necessities. He shook his head and ran a hand over his face. "You have a screw loose."

"More than one." She swallowed hard, gently touching her growing bump. "I knew something was wrong, and I should've listened to my gut, but my hip was throbbing and I was tired. Someone was here and she hit me with a baseball bat."

"She?"

A nod. "Definitely a woman. Told me to back off or die."

"Back off what?"

Her eyes found his. "I think it was Dover."

"What?" Anger fizzed and popped inside him.

Her hand went to the back of her head, gingerly probing around at the base of her skull. "She hit me here first, then across my shoulders to knock me down. My vision blurred, and I couldn't see well. Only caught sight of her legs and boots. Tried to twist so I could catch her face, but she whacked me in the head again."

"Why do you think it was her?"

"My attacker wore camo pants and black boots, just like her."

"That bitch." Caleb made a fist and shoved off the cot to stand. He should case the place, see if she was still around. If Josie hadn't looked like death warmed over, he would. He couldn't leave her. "How did she find you?"

Josie shrugged. "No idea."

He paced to the doorway before wheeling to come back. "Someone from the movie set alerted her. I bet it was that bastard Tyler. What do you wanna bet he did more than recognize her?"

"Still doesn't explain how she could've known I lived here. She doesn't even know who I am."

He eased down beside her again. "Are you sure about that? What is it with you and Pember? How do you know so much about this movie he's shooting?"

A heavy sigh issued from her lips, her gaze darting away. "Being homeless is not the worst of my issues."

He made a whirling motion with his finger for her to go on. Although she wasn't looking at him, she understood.

"Pember stole my script."

"Your what?"

"My screenplay. After my injury, while I was in rehab, I started writing journal entries. Then, as I was recalling different descriptions and dialogue, it sort of morphed in to a movie in my mind. I was trying to distance myself from all the emotions that I went through after I was wounded and while I was trying to find help. It wasn't enough, and pretending that I was writing a story about someone else allowed me to work through many of my issues while not allowing them to overwhelm me."

He was dumbfounded. "You wrote a movie script?"

"When the doctors decided they'd done all they could for me and that I had to live with this, I felt hollow. Just, empty. The pain killers started numbing me out, and I had to do something before I went down a very dark road with them. I'm all Bruno has, and I couldn't let myself check out like that. My script was rough, and I started hanging out at the coffee shop, hoping those that frequented the place might inspire me."

"That's where you saw Pember."

She stared at the floor. "I started learning about scriptwriting techniques, took several online courses. I managed to connect with Glen. I told him about it and he was excited. A female helicopter pilot injured behind enemy lines who had to survive for a couple weeks on her own before she was rescued was the kind of material he was looking for in a movie. You can probably guess the rest."

The fizzle and pop of his previous anger turned to full-on fireworks. "He stole your script."

She straightened out her lower legs, wiggling her toes. "And apparently changed my name to Latoya."

He didn't know if he was more pissed at Pember for cheating her, or at her for not confiding in him earlier. "Where are your pants?"

She glanced up. "There's a locker room and showers down around the corner. My clothes are in there."

"Stay here. I'll be back."

"How did you find me?"

In the doorway, he turned. "There's a lot about me you don't know yet either. I'm taking you to the hospital, so if there's anything else you need, you better tell me where it is so I can grab it."

She pushed to her feet, one hand going to the desk to steady herself. "No hospital, and you have to go after Dover."

She was in no condition to argue, but hell if she wasn't doing it anyway. "You may have a concussion. You *are* going to the hospital."

She took a step forward, shaking her head. "I probably do, but it's mild. I need fluids and someone to wake me every few hours tonight, but other than that, there's nothing a doctor can do for me."

She knew more about medical stuff than he did, but he still hated the idea of not having her checked out properly. "Fine. We'll skip the emergency room, but you're coming home with me."

NINETEEN

She expected a bachelor pad. Instead, she found a small cozy house with signs of Caleb written all over it.

Surfboards leaning against the brick structure. A scattering of flowers and cacti lined a sidewalk that led to the front entrance. She imagined his mother helping him plant those, a smattering of pink and yellow blooms making her smile even through the pain.

A big brass knocker in the shape of an anchor was on the door, and he didn't use a key to let them in, pressing a combination lock before ushering her inside.

The bright interior was cheerful but made her squint. Her head hurt and her shoulders ached, fighting with her hip for attention. The foyer and dining area were all open, a kitchen behind the large wood and glass table that he set her stuff on. As she took a seat at the breakfast bar, he went to the fridge and pulled out a bottled water, setting it on the counter for her. "If you want something stronger, I've got soda or an energy drink."

Because he knew alcohol was out of the question. "This is fine. Thank you."

"You hungry?"

She wasn't, the big meal they'd had still holding her over. Plus, when she was in a lot of pain, food wasn't all that attractive. "I'm good."

His phone rang and he answered it, grabbing her things after he stuck the cell between his ear and shoulder. He motioned her to follow, and she barely listened to his end of the conversation as they traveled to the opposite side where there were two small bedrooms and a bathroom.

Sounded like Joe from the snatches she heard. He'd called him and Coop before they left the hangar, telling them to get eyes on it.

His spare room wasn't made up, the bed bare of linens, and a desk filled with assorted electronics and files. He dropped her bags on the floor and vanished into the hall. She heard the creak of a closet door and then he was back with linens and a blanket. He finished his call and slipped his phone into his pocket before beginning to sheet the bed.

She made an attempt to help, and he told her to sit at the desk and be still. It was a relief since she was so tired her limbs shook like Jell-O.

Underneath his calm, she sensed the rage she'd seen in the bar tightly contained. She was afraid for Glen Pember, but then she remembered what an asshole he was, and decided not to worry about him.

"No luck at finding Dover?"

"She's in the wind again."

The real reason she didn't want Caleb to hunt Glen down was because the man making the bed for her had become an important person in her life. She didn't want him to get in trouble over a bottom feeder like Glen.

They didn't say much, but as Caleb left, he kissed her forehead. "I'll check on you in a couple hours and wake you if you're asleep. Bathroom's across the hall."

She thanked him, but she wasn't sure he even heard her. The call had been important, and she hated the fact he was going to be babysitting her instead of chasing down Dover, but at this point, she literally had nothing left. She crawled onto the mattress and fell asleep instantly.

When she woke some time later, shadows fell softly across her. It took her a moment to remember where she was, but she was so grateful for the soft bed and pillow, she rolled around for a minute and stretched, enjoying it.

Stiffness had crept into her shoulders while she slept, but her hip felt better. If she could get rid of the nagging headache, she might feel almost normal. At least, for her.

She relieved her bladder and washed up. Rifling through her bag, she found her brush and gently worked her tangled hair, examining the lump on the side of her head. There didn't seem to be any permanent damage, and she was thankful for that. No dizziness or nausea and her pupils looked natural. She was even hungry.

She padded from the bathroom and found Caleb spread out on a couch, laptop on the table in front of him, cell in hand. He glanced up when she entered and gave her a smile that didn't quite reach his eyes. "I'll call you back," he said before disconnecting and tossing it on the cushion next to him. "How do you feel?"

"Better. Thank you. Any luck?"

In his lap was a collection of papers bound on the edge. He absentmindedly flipped through them. "Not yet."

Her breath caught in her throat as she realized it included slug lines. "What is that?"

He closed and held it up so she could see the title. "Got my hands on a copy. You wrote this?"

The tightness in her chest grew and she fought to get enough oxygen in her lungs. "Where did you get it?"

He set the script down. "He stole your goddamned movie screenplay. What are you going to do about it?"

Forcing air into her lungs, she ignored the fear and anger burning in her stomach. "I need a lawyer, but as if you may have guessed, I can't afford one at the moment."

Caleb stood, tossing it on the coffee table. He came to stand in front of her, putting his hands on her arms. "I'm gonna get you that attorney, and we're going to sue his ass."

She swallowed hard. "Caleb…I can handle this. You don't need to get involved."

"I already am, damn it. I am going to help you with this."

Her body moved on its own accord, reaching for him. He wrapped his arms around her as she looked up into his face. "What about Dover? We're almost out of time."

"Harris will have to pull Mann from his undercover op. We're still on her trail, but it's gone cold. For now, there's not much else we can do."

Josie felt her stomach sink. "But all those other undercover agents –"

Caleb put a finger to her lips. "It's out of our hands. The taskforce and the head of the West Coast FBI are doing what they can to circumvent the problem. It sucks, but that's life. We can't pull off miracles."

Boy, did she know that. "I'm sorry."

He brushed hair back from her face, his finger tracing her jawline. "You have nothing to be sorry for."

Before she could respond, he lowered his mouth to hers.

For once, she leaned in and accepted the fact she needed someone…she needed Caleb.

His grip was firm, supportive, on her lower back. Lips demanding, he worshipped her with them. Her limbs quivered in anticipation, knowing she was about to forget all about her bruises and aching joints.

His chest was firm under her hands, his hips pressing into her. She wove her fingers through his hair, tugged at it to urge him on.

Her shirt came off, his palms cupping her breasts through her bra. He tugged the straps down, baring her skin to his assault.

She shivered and was ready to lie on the couch and let him do anything he wanted to her, but as he licked at her nipple, then sucked it into his mouth, he grabbed her and lifted her.

Her legs automatically wrapped around his taut waist and he carried her, mouth still on her, through the house and into his bedroom.

"We do this right," he ground out as he lay her down on the soft comforter. It smelled like him and she melted into it.

And then he was removing his belt and she came to her knees to assist with his shirt, loving the muscles underneath the soft fabric.

Deft fingers removed her bra and eased her out of her pants. He left her underwear on, sliding his gaze down her body, his fingers roaming over every part of her until one big, warm palm cupped her between the legs.

"You're sure you can handle this?" he asked, using his other hand to slide a lock of hair off her bare shoulder.

She reached for his erection, prominently displayed between them. He groaned as she stroked him from tip to base. "Oh yes. I can."

From his nightstand, he withdrew a condom and slipped it on. She gripped his long length, and he let her work on him as he slipped one finger under her cotton pants. It dipped into her wetness, came back to stroke her sensitive bud.

Her turn to moan.

"I don't want to hurt you," he whispered, his lips sucking at the lobe of her ear. "What position would be best?"

Her mind could barely process the question, she was already so gone in the heat of him, the feel of him steadily rubbing her into ecstasy. "Huh?"

He kissed her lips, teased them with his tongue, his cock bouncing as her strokes became faster, her grip more demanding. "Is it better if you're on top?"

Sounded good to her. At the moment, pretty much any position she could think of was fine and dandy, she just wanted him inside her.

"Or we can just do this," he continued, his thumb getting in on the action.

He urged her folds to part, inserting one finger, then two.

Josie swore under her breath. "I've been looking forward to this for days." She met his gaze, grabbing him now with both hands and squeezing. "I want it all."

"Fuck." He chuckled low and impassioned. His fingers picked up the pace, matching the rhythm of what she was doing to him. "You are my kind of crazy, woman."

In that moment, she agreed. His thumb had her nearly there, her mind spinning out, her vision blurring. "I...want... perks," she said, trying to keep all of this going—this mind-numbing bliss—a little longer.

"Mm hmm," was his only response, his breathing hard and fast. "Anything."

"A...bonus..."

His hips met her cadence with hard thrusts. She would have toppled backward if it weren't for his hand on her lower spine, holding her in place as his fingers sunk deeper. "You got it."

"I...need..."

He teased her bottom lip when she fell silent, her body

moving with his pace. "What, Josie?" he murmured low and husky, taking her to that sweet place she craved. "What do you need?"

"Oh!" The orgasm crashed over her, making her hands tighten on his hardness. Her walls spasmed around his fingers, hips jutting toward him. "You!"

As all his muscles tightened, he withdrew his hand, lifted her once more and thrust himself inside her.

Legs wrapped around his waist, where they fit so perfectly, she cried out his name. Her head fell back in sweet surrender as he came inside her, milking her orgasm for all it was worth.

Supported in his arms, she'd never felt more satisfied. Never felt more at home.

TWENTY

The next morning, Caleb was more determined than ever to set things straight for Josie.

He made breakfast, then made love to her in the kitchen, complete with syrup. Messy, but delicious.

He'd taken her to the drug store near his house and bought her a cushion for her chair and two gel packs she could alternate in the refrigerator to keep the hip inflammation down. She was stiff but happy and didn't argue over him purchasing the items.

At the office, she sat behind the desk with a smile that hinted at her lasciviousness, and he had a damn hard time staying in his seat, running down a new lead on the mysterious Dover.

Thomas Mann was still undercover, against the wishes of Harris and the higher ups. But he'd found Dover's laptop and disabled it unbeknownst to her or anyone else. She might've had backup copies of the list, but if not, this could buy them time.

Caleb had called a buddy to put a lookout on the movie set,

sure that Dover might show up there again. He wanted Coop to get a warrant and search the damn thing, but they had nothing concrete enough to do so.

So far, his friend had not spotted her, but it was the best lead they had at the moment.

When I get my hands on that bitch…

He was going to put the smack down on her and Pember, too.

He heard the front doorbell, and he picked up his empty mug to get a fresh shot. He hadn't gotten much sleep last night thanks to Josie, and his brain was working overtime. He needed extra caffeine.

He'd been afraid he would hurt her, so he'd been extra careful. She'd been vocal enough to let him know when certain positions were uncomfortable, and he'd been happy to accommodate. After each time, he massaged her hip, putting her to sleep.

Praying this wasn't yet another active case for them, he was surprised to see a woman in uniform standing at Josie's desk. She nodded to him and handed an envelope to Josie. "We were informed three of your checks have recently gone missing. Upon investigating, we found they have not been cashed, so those were voided and new ones generated. Apologies for the delay."

Josie sat stunned. "I don't understand."

"Is that the correct P.O. box?" the uniformed officer asked.

Josie glanced at the printed address. "Yes."

"If the previous checks arrive, please destroy them." She laid the envelope on the desk, smartly turned on her heels, and walked out.

Josie swiveled to face Caleb. "You did this?"

"I plead the fifth."

"I told you not to worry about it, that I would take care of it."

He shrugged, only mildly worried about the anger he saw in her eyes. "You can beat me up later at my place."

She started to argue but the bell dinged and they turned in unison to look.

Coop and Ronni barreled through the entrance. Harris looked pissed; Punto looked scared.

"What happened?" Caleb asked before the door swung closed behind them.

"We have a problem," Coop said.

Ronni visibly swallowed, her fingers rubbing a set of car keys. "Thomas is in trouble. Big time."

TWENTY-ONE

"The SOS from Thomas came twenty minutes ago." Ronni tapped at her phone and showed them the screen. "Bobby and Sam were able to determine his location in this area."

Josie leaned closer to get a better look. Caleb moved next to her and did the same.

"I know that place," Josie said. She exchanged a glance with Caleb. "That's the abandoned airfield."

"You've been there?" Cooper asked.

Another silent exchange with Caleb. "I'm familiar with it. The hangar was used for building and repairing helos and other aircraft. Hasn't been deserted for long. There are multiple buildings—do you know which one he's in?"

Ronni shook her head. "Everybody has a silent beacon on their phone they can access in an emergency. We only use it if we're in distress and cannot establish contact with each other."

"It acts like an encrypted device," Cooper told them. "After the earthquake last year, I had it specially designed for my team to keep us in touch if normal communications are down, or if anyone is in trouble and needs backup but can't call."

"It came from the airfield, possibly the central building, but it covers a half mile area and hasn't been able to lock onto his exact designation."

Joe and Malachi both emerged from their offices. "What can we do to help?" Malachi asked.

Cooper glanced out the window. "The rest of my team, along with an FBI emergency rescue unit is on the way. Problem is, we have no idea what kind of trouble Thomas is in. If Ali or some of her henchmen took him to this spot, we assume she's ordered him to be killed. If we can't get to him before that happens, rushing in with sirens blaring and guns waving will sign his death warrant. I'm taking in a select group to get close first, narrow down his location, before the SWAT team makes their presence known."

Josie felt the rush of tension and adrenaline flood her veins. "There's gotta be five different buildings besides the main one." She couldn't believe that Ari, and in turn Dover, could've been coming and going from there without her knowing it. She'd been living there nearly three weeks now, and they might've been right under her nose. "I'm coming with you. I can help you figure it out, and if anyone gets hurt—"

"No way." Caleb set his mug on the desk and looked at Joe and Malachi. "We're going. You're staying."

"I can handle it."

His brothers disappeared into the back, probably to arm themselves. "Josie..."

That warning in his voice told her to back down. But damn it, this was no time to pull the boss card, or the lover one, either. She knew that location better than any of them.

Ronni interceded. "We can use her."

Josie could see the stubbornness in Caleb's expression as he shook his head again. "It's too dangerous. Besides, she's injured."

That lit her up. Now he was going to use her hip against her.

"I see that," Ronni said, eyeing her lump. "You think it was Dover? That she followed you there?"

Her temple was still bruised and sore, but the lump had lessened significantly. "Long story, but yes, it was her. I'd bet my last dollar on it."

Caleb was talking about her hip, and he had good reason to not want her searching the place, but it still sat wrong with her. "I don't have to do anything more than give you some scoop on the best areas for them to be hiding him."

"No time for debate," Coop said, and Josie knew it was directed at Caleb. "Let's get on the road."

Josie rose and took a step toward him, seeing the way he'd bristled. "I know how to handle a gun, and I won't get in the way. Let me do this."

Cooper's phone rang and he stepped back to take the call. Caleb lowered his voice. "One condition."

Josie nodded. "Name it."

"You stay the fuck in the truck."

Reluctantly, she agreed, but it was probably the best place for her considering her injury. "Deal."

BY THE TIME they arrived at the hangar, Josie was glad she'd insisted on coming. They stopped in a wooded area just outside the park and she gave the team the lowdown about the various buildings as they gathered around the hood of Caleb's truck.

She wished she had an actual paper map, but she drew the best one she could on her own. "This was used for maintenance." She tapped another of her hand-drawn models. "This one has an assortment of equipment, including soldering tools."

A look passed between several of them, and Cooper said, "A good place to torture someone."

Josie never thought she'd hope a man *was* being tortured, but the alternative – being dead – was worse.

Caleb ran a hand over his face. He and his brothers, along with the taskforce members were all wearing flack vests and armed to the teeth. Who needed SWAT when these guys were going in? "You think they're trying to get information out of him before they kill him?"

Ronni's skin, normally the color of coffee, was pale. "If they discovered who he really is, yeah. They'll want to know what he's been feeding to us."

Josie's heart went out to her. In that moment, she couldn't imagine if it was Caleb in Thomas' situation. "Then that's where I would start."

Caleb had given her a Glock and it now sat on the seat of the truck. Josie tried not to think about what could happen in the coming moments, especially with her run of bad luck. "The best way to sneak up on it is through this area here." She tapped the map, showing a small fenced in section behind the building filled with various parts from helicopters and planes. There was a single, small-paned window in the back that looked out over it, but the assorted pieces of aircraft, already succumbing to an assortment of weeds, would give them cover.

"Move out," Cooper ordered. He checked his weapon, a mean looking semi-automatic rifle. "Malachi and Caleb, you take the east. Joe and Ronni, you're on the south. Nelson is already in position over here." He tapped Josie's makeshift map. "I'll meet up with him there and we'll come in from the west. Nobody moves except on my command."

They checked their radios and synced their watches. She

saw the determination in all their faces, and she wished like crazy she could run the half a mile to that spot with Caleb, watch his back and keep him safe, but there was just no way. She couldn't run to begin with, and she couldn't keep up with them with her bad leg over that distance, even if it wasn't already irritated from the past twenty-four hours.

Her head was starting to hurt, but she knew it wasn't from the beating Dover had given her. Fear boiled up inside her belly, the hot sting of it racing through her limbs. As everyone began to scatter, she let the map flutter to the ground and grabbed Caleb by the arm.

It startled him, almost as if he'd forgotten she wasn't coming with them. He saw the fear in her eyes and leaned forward to give her a quick kiss. "Don't worry. Stay in the truck. Keep your radio on and listen, but do not freak out and try to join us, no matter what you hear. Got it?"

No reassurance that he would be okay. Only commands. "Caleb, I…" Her throat tried to seal up on her, her mouth going dry. "Please don't die."

He barked a laugh and whopped his vest with his knuckles. It made a heavy thunking noise. "I'm a tank, completely indestructible." He touched his forehead to hers and smiled. "Don't worry."

She bit her bottom lip. "With my run of luck, I don't want it to touch you."

He kissed her then, throwing in a little tongue, as if to tease her. When he broke away, he was grinning, and she could see something in his gaze that made her melt inside. "You're not getting rid of me that easy. I'd say your luck has turned around since you met me, don't ya think?"

He was trying to lighten the mood, give her something to smile about. "Sometimes you're an egotistical piece of work."

"Only sometimes?"

What she wanted to say was *I love you. You are the best thing that's happened to me since I got back and I can't stand to lose you.* That would be the final straw.

He raised a gloved hand and caressed her cheek. "Stay in the truck. Promise me."

"I promise."

With another kiss, he took off with Malachi and Josie watched as they disappeared in the brush.

TWENTY-TWO

Caleb couldn't believe Josie thought her bad luck would rub off on him.

As he followed Malachi and set up position near the building they suspected Mann was being held in, he thought about how his life had changed since he met her. It was a helluva lot better.

She was his good luck charm.

He nestled in the shell of an old Jeep next to his brother and listened to Cooper's soft instructions relaying across the radio on his vest. It was rare they got into a situation like this in their line of work, but Caleb missed the days of engagement with the enemy. Fugitive apprehension still gave him the occasional opportunity to go after criminals, but this? This made his blood heat in a manner he hadn't felt since leaving the Marines.

ICE Agent Nelson Cruz had spotted two vehicles parked several yards away, partially hidden by a large, out of commission tanker truck. One of the garage doors on the building was up, and voices could be heard inside. Cooper alerted the SWAT team waiting for him to give the "go."

For the moment, Coop and Nelson were sneaking closer to try and eavesdrop. Coop had told everyone to hold position until he identified who and what was inside that building.

Malachi peeked over the side of the Jeep and then returned to his spot next to Caleb. He tapped his radio to mute it as he lowered his voice. "You and Josie are for real?"

Caleb continued scanning the area to the south, just to make sure no one could sneak up to take them by surprise. "I've never felt this way about anyone before. She's under my skin, bro."

They fell silent, listening to conversation between Cooper and Ronni. She wanted to disable the vehicles, just to be sure no one escaped. There was a long pause as Cooper considered this, then gave her the go ahead.

In his mind, Caleb imagined the FBI agent cautiously working her way to the vehicles. He wondered how she planned to put them out of action. She couldn't exactly pop the hoods and take out a spark plug.

He bet Josie would have a suggestion or two, and the thought made him smile.

Malachi punched Caleb gently on the shoulder. "Just don't blow it, okay? We don't want to lose her as our office manager. She's completely revamped my tracking spreadsheets. Made the bookkeeping easier, too. I think she's saved me ten hours of work this week."

"Oh, I see how it is." Caleb shot him a grin. "All about you."

From the inside they heard a commotion, and a man yelled a string of curses. His voice was strained, the edge of pain clear.

Caleb and Malachi went still.

He knew that tone, could almost feel the pain in his own body, but he relished it. It fired him up, made the rage inside him bloom, and that's when he knew he was ready.

That kind of emotion played with most people's mental

faculties. The bleed of it in their system made them do stupid things. For him, it was the opposite.

When he felt that heat rip through his system, his mind sharpened, his cognitive abilities focusing and zeroing in on the target with deadly accuracy.

The next several minutes passed with a nervous calm he could only describe as battle-ready.

A sweet crescendo built when Cooper gave instructions and then…the countdown.

Five.

Four.

Caleb pushed from the vehicle's frame.

Three.

He and Malachi exchanged a knowing look. *Be safe. Kick ass. Oorah.*

Two.

One.

"Go, go, go!"

They took the building in waves, Cooper and Nelson going in first.

"Two targets, ten o'clock!" Coop's voice boomed out.

"Got em'," Joe said. A commotion, then, "Two down!"

Ronnie: "Thomas, southwest corner!"

"Target on the move," Joe yelled. "Three o'clock."

Caleb and Malachi entered. "On it," Caleb told the group.

The idiot ran, firing wildly at them with his handgun. Malachi went right and Caleb left, their voices and footfalls echoing in the large building.

The perpetrator raced up a set of metal stairs and Malachi started to fire. Caleb yelled, "No," and signaled he was going after him.

He took them two at a time, wanting to get his hands on the

guy. His feet moved so fast, he felt like he was flying. Gaining, gaining...

At the top, he tackled him, sending both of them to the floor. Below, he heard a new scrimmage erupt, heard the sound of gunfire. Malachi's yell.

Two cars. Four people. All now subdued.

Or were they?

The fight below suggested otherwise.

Not possible.

Cooper and his team were too good. They'd taken the group by surprise.

Unless...

There were more than the three kidnappers and Thomas.

His perp wrestled under him, trying to hit him with the handgun. Caleb pinned him to the ground, knocking it from his hand, and punched him in the face.

More than once.

"Who else is here?"

The man spit at him. His quick reflexes jacked on adrenaline, Caleb jerked back and it missed.

"You so shouldn't have done that," he snarled.

By the third jab, the guy was still conscious, but losing copious blood from his now crooked nose. The fight below had stopped, more voices—probably SWAT—joining in the fun.

Caleb heard the sound of heavy boots clanging on the stairs. He wanted to keep hitting the bastard, reared a fist back to do so.

"Caleb!" Malachi was behind him. "It's over, bro. Ease up."

Josie's face floated in front of him.

The rage flickered out.

"It's all good." He raised his hands. "Broken nose, but that's the least of his worries."

He stood, retrieving the gun as Malachi looked over his handiwork.

"Everyone okay?" Caleb questioned.

Mal hauled the guy to his feet. "There were two more having a smoke in a back room. They came in guns blazing, but the team is okay."

"Oorah."

A fist bump. Together they cuffed and escorted the man down the steps into the main area. The SWAT team was clearing various offshoots of the main building, and as Caleb took stock of the two dead assailants, he was glad to see Mann was alive, even though it appeared he was barely conscious.

Cooper and Ronni worked to break the chains strapping him to a metal table. An assortment of tools they'd used on him lay on the ground. "Dover…" he sputtered, grabbing for Ronni. "Releasing those names."

She shushed him, worrying over his wounds as he seemed to swim in and out of delirium.

Dover was still out there. A ghost in the wind.

But she's been here.

He had no doubt she was the one who'd told Ari about the place. Probably pointed her to this building, in fact, to torture then dispose of Mann's body.

Fuck. What if she'd killed Josie?

Why *hadn't* she?

Because Dover wasn't a killer. She was a gutless, spineless hacker who hid behind her computer and other criminals to get what she wanted.

"Clear!" A SWAT member's voice rang out.

Another from a distant wing answered.

Big fucking place. Lots of areas to hide.

Maybe Josie wasn't the only one using the hangar's abandoned buildings as a hideout. Was it possible their fugitive had also been living here?

"I need to ask Josie something," he said to his brothers. "Back in a minute."

He was sticking his gun in its holster when he saw movement behind Joe. "Get down!"

In the next second, he felt the blow of a bullet hit him square in the chest. The sound of a gun ricocheting echoed in his ears.

Caleb went down.

TWENTY-THREE

Josie screamed.

She'd done as Caleb demanded and stayed in the truck, but as she'd heard SWAT clearing the place, she'd driven over as fast as she could.

Arriving just outside the giant opened door, she'd been so relieved to see Joe, Malachi, and Caleb standing off to one side. She'd thrown it into park, careful to remain out of the way of the various personnel as they rushed inside.

She'd been about to call Caleb's name when she'd heard him call out. In the next second, his body jerked and he fell.

People shouted, guns were drawn, bodies moving into her line of view as she tried to rush forward. Someone grabbed her by the shoulders and yanked her back.

"Let me go!" she yelled, fighting against the man holding her.

He dragged her behind a large drum barrel and forced her to the ground, making her hip scream. "Stay down!"

Anger bursting inside her, she elbowed him, breaking free from his tight grip. She scrambled out, but didn't get far.

A grunt and he latched on to her ankle and jerked, her hip firing again with a sharp stab of pain up into her back.

She used her other foot to kick him and managed to get loose, pain nearly blinding her, but her need to get to Caleb was stronger.

Malachi and Joe, covering Caleb's body, blocked her view as she attempted to run to him. Joe sprang up and jetted toward the spot where the bullet had come from.

Josie fell to her knees, grabbing his shoulders and shaking him. "Oh my god. Caleb! Are you okay?"

Her medical training had her scanning him for blood, but she saw none. She did see a hole in his vest.

Malachi reached over and grabbed her arm. "He's fine."

But he wasn't opening his eyes. She leaned forward, using her fingers to pry open his left and then his right lid. His pupils were dilated. "I don't think so."

Her breathing was ragged and her heart felt like it was going to beat out of her chest. "Caleb." She shook him again. "Come on. Wake up!"

He groaned and a grin split his lips, his left eye peeking open. "Like I said earlier, you can't get rid of me that easy, Josie."

Relief mixed with irritation bubbled inside her. She punched his arm. "You asshole!"

"Come on, buttercup. You weren't worried, were you?"

Her eyes stung with tears. "Are you really all right?"

He raised a hand to rub the back of his head. "I will be once the room stops spinning. I whacked my noggin pretty good. Give me a sec."

His eye fluttered closed again and she nearly fell over his chest in relief as sobs wracked her body.

Malachi patted her on the back before standing. Joe returned, shaking his head. "Did anyone see who it was?"

The responses were all negative, Caleb's included. "I saw an arm, a flash of light on the gun. That's all."

Malachi, Joe, and Cooper began discussing who the assailant might have been...another straggler in the group?

The SWAT team wasn't done clearing all the hidey holes. Who else might be inside?

She didn't care at this point, as long as Caleb was okay.

"Hey."

His voice brought her gaze up and she dashed at the wetness on her cheeks. Staring at her, he reached to smooth her hair. "The vest stopped the bullet. Really, I'm good. You might have to check me for a concussion, though."

In the distance, she heard the ambulance siren. Coop had put them on standby in case they were needed.

Caleb grinned again, waggled his eyebrows. "Guess I better stay at your place tonight."

The SWAT commander strode across the open space. "You piss your pants there, Cahill?"

Caleb shot him the finger. "Might not have happened if your guys were doing your job, Butch."

Butch winked at Josie, then told Coop, "Everything's clear. No more surprises."

Caleb angled himself up slowly with her help until he was in a seated position. She checked the back of his head and he whined like a child when she hit the sore spot. Before she could do anything else, Ronni was beside her. "EMTs are almost here, but I wondered if you could look at Thomas. He's in bad shape."

The woman's voice broke as she said it, and Josie could see she was trying to be strong through her fear. "Of course."

When she turned back to Caleb, he waved her off. "Go."

Thomas was indeed a mess. It looked bad because of all the blood and the burn marks, but what she was most concerned about was shock setting in. "I need blankets," she yelled to no one in particular. "Anything to warm him up."

As people piled on an assortment of jackets and other clothes, since no one had a blanket in the summer in San Diego, she stopped the worst of the wounds from bleeding, and tried to reassure Ronni he would be okay.

As the EMTs administered an IV and got Thomas on the gurney, Josie overheard Ronni tell Caleb, "You've got a great woman there. Don't blow it."

Ronni left in the ambulance by Thomas' side. Caleb, grimacing next to her, put his arm around her. "You did good today."

"You should've gone to the hospital, too."

"No way. I've got my private nurse right here."

"What about the other agents?" she asked as they stood in the open doorway and watched the ambulance grow smaller in the distance. "What about Dover?"

He hugged her close. "Everything will work out. Don't worry about them."

Josie turned in his arms, praying he was right.

TWENTY-FOUR

It was no hardship to look after Caleb that evening.

His head seemed as hard as ever, no bruise or swelling, but the smack on it had knocked the stubbornness from him.

He did have a growing bruise on his left pectoral. Playing up the pity, he encouraged Josie to care for it repeatedly while they spent the night wrapped in each other's arms.

According to Harris, the captured men weren't talking. Thomas was in serious condition, but his prognosis was good. He'd been conscious enough to tell Cooper he hadn't given up anything while under duress. He had no idea how Ari had figured out who he was, and all guesses involved Dover.

Caleb was sure she was the one who'd clipped him, and he was more determined than ever to hunt her down before she disappeared forever.

Thomas also told them Ari was meeting with a new international buyer for her stolen art—an unexpected black-market entity who'd taken a sudden interest in her goods. Selling the names of undercover agents had fallen low on her list at the moment, but was still of vital concern to the FBI, DEA, and ATF.

The following morning, the Cahill brothers met with Cooper and his taskforce.

Ronni, Sam, Nelson, and the computer guru, Bobby, gathered around the conference table at the Bondsman Brothers' office. Everyone had coffee in front of them, thanks to Josie, but no one was drinking.

"We need to fan out over San Diego," Caleb told them. "Dover Garnet has been seen at a movie production lot not far from here, and we believe she's who attacked Josie two nights ago."

"And shot you," Ronni added with venom in her voice.

"I don't see her as a killer," Caleb stated, playing with a pen. "But could be. Whoever it was knew the layout of the hangar buildings and that's why they got away. It's possible she's been using the place as a hideout. Also, her boyfriend, Pember's, trailer on the set. I doubt she'll go back to either at this point, but she's running out of places to hide."

Bobby, in an electric wheelchair, sat at one end. He swung a laptop around to show them camera footage on the screen. "She went in to Legends Coffee Bar downtown this morning."

A muscle in Caleb's jaw twitched.

She was wearing a wig, hat, and sunglasses, so she probably assumed the regulars wouldn't recognize her.

"Not too smart," Josie said under her breath.

"You think she's meeting someone?" This from Caleb.

Cooper sat forward. "Who?"

Caleb pointed at her. "Tell them what you know."

Everyone's attention now focused on her. She gave them a brief rundown, forcing herself to breeze through the personal aspects, and saw the taskforce members considering this new information.

Ronni was upset about the theft of her script; Josie assured her it would be dealt with.

Sam sipped her coffee. "What would make Dover risk going there now?"

Josie shrugged. "Love. If she was looking for Glen, she might've chanced it."

Bobby turned his screen back around. "Good thing the FBI's facial recognition system was able to pick her out."

"Why not go to the set?" Joe questioned no one in particular.

"Why not just call or text him?" Ronni added.

Caleb tapped his pen on a notepad. "She knows we've made the connection, so she assumes we're watching Glen."

Josie nodded. "And maybe he's not answering his phone."

Sam studied the liquid in her cup. "She's gotten in so deep with Ali, she could blow everything for him, too. He's cut her out."

"But she still loves him." Josie saw it playing out inside her head. "She still needs him."

"For what?" Cooper seemed perplexed.

Josie leaned over and studied the paused video on Bobby's laptop. "If Ali's unhappy with her, especially because she let Thomas get into their ranks, Dover may be scared. She blew it by letting a suspected agent get close to the cartel leader. It's quite possible one of the reasons Ali recruited her in the first place was to investigate anyone she hires."

Agreement went around the table with a variety of head nods.

"So she really is running out of spots to hide," Bobby said. "She may have already headed for the border, afraid Ali's after her as well as the rest of us."

"Not if she believes she has a chance with Glen," Josie argued.

"Or he has something of hers she wants before she bails," Caleb offered.

Another round of nods.

"How do we flush this bitch out?" Ronni asked.

Josie took a big sip and swallowed past her fear. "I have an idea."

TWENTY-FIVE

"Y ou wanna be bait?" Caleb's voice was flat, incredulous.

She'd laid down a very hasty, and quite honestly, sketchy plan to flush out Dover by using Glen.

"Worth a try, isn't it?" She toyed with her cup. "He's our link to her. She's no doubt got his phone, computer, email, everything tapped, under her control. If I make contact and threaten him, it may lure her to us."

Sam looked like she was warming to the idea. "Especially if she has a protective streak for him, or like Caleb mentioned, he has something she wants before she leaves town. I think it's worth a try, too."

Several discussions broke out at the same time, most seeming to dismiss the plan. Josie raised her hand to get everyone's attention and they all fell silent. "There's no way that this group can canvas all of San Diego and find her, even if she is running out of places to hide. This plan may have a chance. We have to attempt it."

Sam was the only one that was on her side. For the next

half hour, different schemes were tossed about, but each one was successfully dismissed. With some satisfaction, Josie sat back while they hashed things out and finally came back around to her idea.

Cooper rose, finally taking a drink of his coffee, before setting the cup down with authority. "All right, I'll okay you threatening Pember. Where are you doing this and when?"

Josie took a minute to think it over. "My place, and as soon as we can get there, I guess." Cooper seemed as if he wanted more. She planted her feet and gave him a direct stare. "Dover's already come after me once, and she knew about the hangar, which is probably how Ali knew. If nothing else, threatening Glen might make her show just to shut me up. She did tell me to back off or die."

Sam touched her arm. "Are you sure you want to try this? If she's now on the run from Ali, and Pember is avoiding her, she may act like a cornered animal."

"I'll be okay. Caleb will make sure of it."

Cooper glanced at the single picture hanging on the wall and put his hands on his hips. "My team will be standing by. We want this woman as badly as you."

Malachi stood and reached to shake Cooper's hand. "As soon as we have everything in place, I'll let you know. We'd welcome your assistance, and will be happy to turn our fugitive over to you when we capture her."

The meeting disbanded, and Josie began collecting the cups. Sam and Joe helped, as Malachi and Caleb walked Harris and his team to the door.

After they'd left and Josie came out of the kitchen, Caleb grabbed her and pulled her aside. "You don't have to do this."

"Yes, I do. I know you don't like it, but we're going to stop Dover and Glen."

.   .   .

AN HOUR LATER, they were at the hangar, everyone in place under Caleb's instructions.

Josie sat behind the desk, her cell lying on top. Caleb checked in with everyone standing by, and ran through the possible scenarios with them.

Finally, he stared at her and pointed his finger. "We're a go when you are."

Josie opened her contacts and found the number Glen had given her months ago when he'd been helping her. Her hands were sweating as she heard it connect, the ringing on the other end. She held her breath, waiting for him to pick up, but the call went to voicemail.

A part of her was slightly relieved, the other disappointed. When the buzz sounded for her to leave her message, she cleared her throat. "Glen, it's Josie Jackson. I've been on the set; I have a copy of the script. I know what you're doing and I've hired a lawyer. Cease and desist with the filming, because I'm coming after you. You've rushed this through, after stealing my life story, and I'm going to take down your entire empire. You know what I'm talking about, and I have the proof. If you want to talk to me in person, here's the address."

She rattled it off. "You have until midnight to contact me or come here. If you don't, then tomorrow morning my attorney and I will hold a press conference. We will destroy you and everyone associated with this movie."

Josie hung up.

Then they waited.

TWENTY-SIX

J osie woke to a *thumpthumpthump* overhead.

Instantly, she was transported to her time in the Army and the noise of her helicopter.

It was a sound that thrummed in her blood with passion, but it also triggered the last memory she had as an officer, her weeks of survival flashing through her brain rapid fire and haunting.

Not another nightmare.

There'd been a lot of those, but not many recently. Shaking in the cool air, she forced her eyelids open and gained her bearings.

The soft glow from a lantern came from the desk, and she saw Caleb asleep in the chair, one of the cats curled in his lap. His feet were up, chin slumped against his collarbone.

The helicopter faded in the distance, probably the Marines or Navy running an early morning exercise in the desert. They woke her every once in a while.

With shaking hands, she scooped back her hair and adjusted herself on the cot. Her hip was burning with a dull ache, and she probably should have spent the night on the floor, once it was apparent nothing was going to happen.

Lucky for her, Caleb had been more than happy to rub it, her thighs, and back. The strength and gentleness in his hands had relaxed her so much, she'd fallen asleep.

Checking her phone, she saw it was just after four. The sun would be rising soon. On one hand, she was relieved she hadn't missed any calls from Glen, but on the other, disappointment welled in her chest.

Her bait hadn't worked, and with the approaching dawn, she wondered if Cooper and his team were still watching and waiting. She felt regret that she'd made them stay out there all night. At least here inside, she and Caleb had traded stories, played cards, and then he'd given her that fantastic massage.

Watching him rest was a balm to the disappointment. Seeing the cat at home on him made her smile. Hers had been restless, but at least she'd gotten some, and while the rude awakening wasn't welcome, she was ready to tackle the day and do whatever she could to help resolve this case.

Where are you, Dover?

Shifting to sit up, she gingerly rubbed her hip bone. She needed to relieve her bladder and wash her face.

Her movements startled Caleb awake—not what she'd planned. She'd hoped to kiss him so, but now he sat forward, feet hitting the floor and scaring the cat. He reached for the gun laying on the desk, the poor feline screeching a meow as she tore to the closed door. "What is it? What happened?"

Josie opened it so she could escape and smiled at him. "We both fell asleep."

"Shit." He rubbed grit from his eyes. "No calls?"

She shook her head. "Do you think Cooper and his team are still here?"

Caleb blew out a deep sigh as he slumped back into the

chair. He laid the weapon down and picked up the walkie talkie, thumbing it to raise Cooper. "Any sightings?"

"Good morning to you, too, sunshine. Nothing to report. How much longer do you want us on duty? Got some grumpy agents here."

The taskforce leader usually sounded gruff, but he came off downright hellish at the moment. Josie needed to buy all of them coffee.

Caleb hit the mic button. "It's a bust. You guys might as well pack it up. Josie and I will head to the office and call you if we get any more leads or have further ideas."

"Roger that."

Josie waved her thumb toward the hallway. "I'm going to hit the bathroom and wash up. Then I need copious amounts of strong coffee."

Caleb yawned and nodded. "Ditto." He rocked forward coming to his feet and tucked the gun into the back of his waistband.

"I'm sorry it didn't work," Josie said as they made their way to the locker room and showers. She'd been bluffing, of course, and had no lawyer, nor a clue how to arrange a press conference.

Caleb touched her hip. "How is it?"

Outside the windows, the sun was beginning to kiss the sky, lifting the purple shadows. "Still a little sore after being manhandled by that SWAT guy, but you made it a lot better last night. I think if I could sleep for twelve hours and just rest, I'd feel tons better. It would also help if I could get Dover for you."

He left his hand on her as they walked, the warmth seeping into her skin through her shirt and yoga pants. "You have great ideas, so keep them coming. This is part of it. We keep throwing things against the wall until something sticks and we get a tiny thread that leads us to the person we're hunting."

They hit the women's and she peeled off, pushing the automatic door open as he went farther to the men's. Inside she went about her business, stepping quickly under the spray and wishing Caleb was with her. There was no hot water, though, so probably better to save that kind of play for his place.

Her face in the mirror over the sink showed her how pale she was, how ragged looking. Dark circles hung under her eyes like bruises. Her skin was sallow.

There was a part of her that felt defeated, and yet, thanks to Caleb, she still held an inner strength and hope. If they could just stop Dover before she released those names, Josie would take that as a win. Even if she never got revenge on Glen, or the taskforce nabbed Ali, that one small thing could save dozens of people.

When she exited, Caleb was waiting for her. He pushed from where he'd been leaning and took her hand. "I'm gonna grab the truck. I'll swing by and pick you up. While I'm gone, I want you to stay in that office with the door locked, and I'll leave you the gun."

He'd left the truck in the lot next to the park and walked to the building the previous evening. She assumed Cooper's team had done a similar thing, so they wouldn't be spotted and scare off Dover or anyone else who might show. She was grateful not to have to trek all that way and squeezed his hand. "There's a couple things I want to pack while you're gone."

He shot her a grin. "Oh yeah? You moving out?"

"I don't care if I have to covertly sleep at the office, or in your truck, I'm not staying here any longer. I will have to return to check on the cats and feed them. Once I cash my checks, I want to start capturing them one by one and taking them in to get fixed. Most are too feral to ever be adopted and kept in indoors, but I still want to stop them from reproducing and contributing more to overpopulation."

At the entrance to the office, he kissed her forehead. "You're staying at my place. Don't argue."

She leaned on the jamb and gave him a quizzical expression. "Are you asking me to live with you? You barely know me, and what you've seen so far isn't exactly couple material, is it?"

He laughed. "Actually, I was thinking the opposite. I'm pretty sure you're one of the best things that's ever happened to me, and I'm pretty scared that you'll take off. I'm hoping if you move in, I can convince you to stay."

Her heart felt like it would burst. "You really scared me yesterday. I hope the majority of your apprehensions aren't that dangerous."

One of the cats strolled down the hallway, flicking its tail. It sauntered close, but still kept its distance, and meowed at her. That was the hungry signal. Caleb squeezed her hand again. "I'll go get the truck. Stay in like I told you, okay?"

She agreed and he handed her the weapon before he jogged off.

Inside, she left the entry open for a minute as she used a can opener. The sound brought everybody running, and as soon as she had the felines, she shut and locked the door. They inhaled the food, a couple of the more affectionate ones rubbing against her ankles and allowing her to pet them. She began gathering the few items she had stored here, putting them in her rucksack.

Several meowed to be let out, and she considered doing it, but forced herself to sit at the desk and wait for Caleb. Since she was sure that there was no one here but her, it was hard to follow orders, but no way was she going to be blindsided by Dover or anyone else again.

She played with her phone, returning a text to Bruno and letting him know she was fine. He'd been out of town on an assignment and was disappointed he'd missed the previous day's fun.

She was deep into a conversation with him, when over the sound of the crying cats, she heard a knock. Was Caleb back already?

She came to her feet, grabbing the gun and taking off the safety. She didn't say a word, moving toward the door and trying to listen, which was impossible with the cats howling.

It came again, more forceful this time, and standing so close, she knew it wasn't from a fist.

It was wood on wood.

Shit. Josie backed away, raising the gun and pointing it.

Dover was here.

This time, Josie was ready.

The cats continued caterwauling and she tried to shoo them from her feet, taking a solid stance. Pulse racing, she aimed at the door, a trickle of sweat dripping down her temple.

"I know you're in there," came the woman's voice. "Open up and let's get this over with."

Yep, Dover.

Josie had to clamp her teeth together not to answer.

Stay focused. Don't let her taunt you into doing something rash.

Caleb would be back any minute, she only needed to hold her off until then.

She glanced at the desk, looking for the radio, but Caleb must've taken it with him. She grabbed her cell with one hand and dialed him, putting it on speakerphone so she could return both hands to the gunstock.

Without warning the bat hit the metal doorknob once, twice, a third time. It jumped, giving under the brute force.

The cats scattered, fleeing for cover under the desk and cot.

Josie prayed the lock would hold, the knob, too. It was hardly an expensive set, and her side began to loosen more as the beating continued.

Whack

Whack

Whack

Overhead, Josie heard a helicopter, the thump of blades mixing with the bat noises. Memories swamped her, making her vision blur and her heart race.

Not now!

The noise was too loud in her ears, the scene playing out in front of her involving injured men and the bang and report of weaponry.

She had to move, had to get out. Where to go?

The door burst open, bringing her back into the present moment and she jerked, tripping on one of the cats.

Dover stood in the doorway, chunks of the bat broken, but still enough of it in one piece as she smiled at Josie. "Thought you were going to trick Glen in to coming here? Sorry, he's not that stupid."

The trip caused her to twist her ankle and shooting pain flooded up into her spine. The chopper outside nearly drowned out the words. Cats sprinted out the door, others cowered in place.

Josie leaned her damaged hip against the shelving unit behind her and continued to point at Dover. "I'm not alone, and you're about to—"

Dover tossed the bat down and pulled out a gun. She locked it on Josie's face. "Looks like we have a Mexican stand-off. But I guarantee you, only one of us is walking out of here."

Josie slowed her breathing, sighting down the barrel and prepared to pull the trigger.

Caleb appeared behind Dover. "Stop!"

Dover whirled and fired.

TWENTY-SEVEN

"Caleb!" Josie yelled. "No!"

Caleb staggered and fell to his knees, the hole in his belly leaking hot blood like a faucet.

Gut shot. Of all the things.

The son of a bitch burned. Josie rushed to him, her gun still trained on Dover, trying to force the woman away. "Get back!"

"Drop it or I'll shoot him again, and you as well," Dover threatened.

Dots flashed in the corners of his vision. He fell, the floor hard under him. Josie moved to stand between him and Dover. "I'm going to shoot you on principle," she threatened.

Bam! The loud echo of the weapon slammed into his already ringing ears.

Dover saw it coming, and dodged. She laughed like a deranged woman. "Nice. Didn't think you had it in you."

Caleb knew she had no intention of leaving him or Josie alive, and he sensed Josie knew it, too. He was on hands and knees now, dragging in stifled breaths as he tried to gain his feet, digging deep for that rage that was always driving him forward. He searched for it, clawed for it.

And came up empty.

"Stay with me," she demanded, and he knew she was speaking to him. To Dover, she said, "You might be surprised at what I'm willing to do."

He had to save her, no matter what, but his body refused to cooperate. He grabbed for anger at Dover, at himself, but mostly it was cold fear biting at him like a rabid dog. Fear of losing Josie forever because he hadn't done his job.

Another shot rang out and he could no longer tell who was shooting. "Jo...sie..."

There was yelling and he sensed someone else entering the room, but his vision turned into a shadowy black and white. What he saw was limited as the edges of his eyesight kept growing darker and darker.

He wasn't sure how or when, but he ended up flat on his face, his nose striking the hard concrete floor.

He heard Josie yell his name again. She was no longer in view. A pair of feet he didn't recognize came to stand in front of him. "He'll be dead shortly," a woman's voice said. She had a European accent his fuzzy brain couldn't quite place.

Was this the infamous Ali Karo?

"You...bitch..." he murmured.

With all his strength, he tried to force his body up, but his arms and legs were numb. He couldn't control them. The sticky warmth of his blood coated his shirt.

She took one high-heeled foot and pushed the point into his shoulder. "We'll let him live long enough to watch his girlfriend die."

As she walked away, Caleb saw Dover pressing Josie's face against the wall, a gun resting at the back of her skull. "Maybe I should move her a little closer then."

Suddenly Josie was shoved across the room and fell in front of Caleb. "Do not die on me," she murmured.

"Get on with it," Ali said in her thick speech. "We have a lot of things yet to accomplish today. Don't screw this up like before."

Caleb's vision drew to a pinpoint, Josie becoming a tiny circle of light. He tried to convey what he was thinking, and it had nothing to do with Dover or Ali.

I love you.

He tried to make his lips work, but only gurgling noises came out. Josie was crying, yelling at him to keep his eyes open, to look at her. That she was going to save him.

I love you.

"Just so you know, I plan to kill Glen, too," Dover stated. "He's nothing but a cheater."

Josie was leaning close, her face only inches from his. She sobbed loudly.

Then she winked at him.

In the next second, she kicked her bad leg through the air, aiming for Dover's boots. She hooked an ankle, then Dover hit the ground on her side, a surprised *oomph* forced from her lungs.

The gun clattered to the floor.

Ali yelled, but Josie was already on it, rolling and coming up on a knee like an action star.

Bambambam.

The rapid blasts echoed through the room.

Adrenaline shot through his veins and he blinked away the shadows. Ali fell back, stumbling on Josie's cane. She hit the desk, cartwheeling onto the floor. Josie stood, leaving Caleb's line of sight again. He knew he didn't have much left, but his fingers walked out, reaching for her.

Although his hearing was growing as dim as his vision, he heard the pounding of boots and the sound of Cooper's voice.

The cavalry was here.

Relief.

He blacked out and when he came to, Josie was next to him, flipping him over and yelling orders at people.

As he faded in and out of consciousness, he endured pressure on the wound on his stomach, sensed himself being hoisted onto a cot. Warm autumn air kissed his cold cheeks.

The next thing he knew, he was being lifted into the air, the *whomping* of blades above him like a bass drum, blocking out all other noise.

Although he couldn't see her, he knew who was flying him from the hangar. Caleb closed his eyes and let the shadows take him.

"CALEB!" A chilly hand smacked his cheek, and he wanted to yell at her to stop, to let him sleep. His body was on fire, but Josie didn't relent. "Open your damned eyes. I know you're faking it, rosebud. Do *not* think you get to die and leave me in this mess!"

He was able to crack his lids open and see her running beside him as he was wheeled into what must've been a hospital. His body was jangled as they crossed a threshold, white lab-coated folks calling instructions and telling Josie she needed to back away so they could do their job.

She said obscene things that made him smile through the pain, and kept her spot beside him. "I didn't fly you here so you could die." Her voice was the no-nonsense nurse he'd heard a few times now. "Where's the brawler I met at Bad Medicine? I need you to fight, Caleb. Fight for your life. Fight for *me*."

She was covered in blood. Hers? His? Everything was blurring, and he couldn't remember exactly what had happened. What day it was.

But she was holding his hand, and he felt a surge of strength. He sent every bit of it into his fingers to tighten them as much as he could. "I...love..."

"I know. Now shut up." She squeezed back. "I'll be waiting for you when you get out of surgery. Fight, Caleb."

In his mind, he promised he would.

Once more, his eyes drifted shut, his last view that of her beautiful, worried face.

TWENTY-EIGHT

onni found Josie pacing, waiting a bit of a distance from Caleb's family. "Thank you," she said, handing the woman a cup of coffee from the vending machine.

Josie accepted it but didn't drink. "For what?"

"For what you did to help Thomas, of course."

She leaned on the wall, staring toward the surgical suite. "How is he?"

Her heart wasn't in the question. It was with Caleb behind those doors.

Ronni knew the feeling. She had it every time Thomas went undercover. He was so damn good at it; couldn't and wouldn't give it up. She wanted to ask him to, but never did. He loved her even more than the job—and that was saying something—and she would never clip his wings like that. "He'll have a few new scars, but he'll recover."

"Good."

Dead. No emotion.

Ronni knew that defense, too. A barrier she'd learned to put up around herself to protect her heart. "He'll make it."

Josie's flat gaze swung to hers. Behind the defense, Ronni sensed the fear and love she had for the man. "How do you... How do you know?"

Ronni tapped her skull. "He's too hardheaded to die. Trust me. It takes a special type of person to handle what we all do on a daily basis. Caleb and his brothers are tough. I get the sense you are, too."

"I thought I was." She looked at the floor, blew out a sigh of air between her lips. "I mean, I am. Normally. I've been through a lot in my life. I'm no quitter, but this..."

Her focus trailed to the doors again.

Ronni gave her arm a squeeze and jabbed her chin toward the others. "You've got family, JJ. Put that fear to work and go support them. Let them do the same for you."

The elevator across the way dinged and Bruno stepped out. "Josie." He rushed to her and nodded at Ronni. "Are you okay?"

Ronni let go of Josie's arm and let Bruno engulf her in a hug.

"I'm fine, it's Caleb."

Her eyes filled with tears and Bruno set her back and held her shoulders with his big hands, as if to reassure her. "Don't worry about him. He'll be bugging the shit out of both of us before we can blink."

Ronni smiled, seeing Cooper scanning the hall for her. "I have to get back to Thomas," she told the brother and sister. "Thanks, again, Josie."

Josie held out a hand and they gave each other a reassuring squeeze. "I'll check on you soon."

Ronni winked. "Go be with your family. We'll catch up later."

Josie gave her a sad smile, and let Bruno lead her to the waiting area.

JOSIE PACED the floor for another hour cooling her heels till Caleb got out of surgery and recovery.

Malachi, Joe, Sam, and Mr. and Mrs. Cahill joined her. Every once in a while, one of them talked about him, and sometimes they shared a laugh. Sam and Josie made sure there was water and coffee constantly flowing.

Bruno had delivered Dover to the county jail before he'd arrived. Her paperwork had been processed.

A surgeon eventually emerged to explain the extent of Caleb's injury, but all she heard were the unsaid words—it had been hit and miss during the operation; Caleb had a long haul in front of him.

The family went first to see him in intensive care. When she was finally admitted in to his hospital room while his parents took a break, she fought back tears. This wasn't her Caleb—the man in the bed was too pale, too still.

Joe and Malachi stepped out to give her privacy, Sam hugging her before she went to Joe's side. Josie sat next to him, watching his eyes move under the lids until the anesthesia began wearing off. The cut on his cheek that she had doctored was going to be a scar, but the red line was such a minor thing now.

"Hey, buttercup," he said. His words were slurred, as if his mouth was filled with cotton.

She kissed his cheek before settling her chin in one hand as she leaned on the railing. "How do you feel?"

A loopy grin. "I don't feel anything."

She patted his hand. "Good. Just sleep."

"You're moving in." His words sounded like a drunk's, lifting and falling. "Stay with me..."

"I'm not going anywhere."

"Forever."

Although they'd had a similar conversation that morning, she told herself that this was just the drugs. "You need to focus on getting your strength back. Lots of rest. We'll talk about our future together once you're stronger."

He fell asleep, woke a few minutes later, and asked her about moving in with him again. She leaned down and stared him in the eyes. "Are you messing with me?"

He gave her a clear look, this time his words devoid of the drugs. "Promise me. You're going to stay with me forever."

"Caleb, you've just been through a very serious injury and operation. What you need to do right now is –"

"What I *need* is to know you're not going to run away from this." He heaved a noisy sigh. "That you're not blaming yourself for what happened."

That cut close to the truth and she flinched. "You have to stop pretending that I'm not bad luck. I don't know what I did in a past life to cause all of this crap to happen, but it's just plain fact. I'm spiraling out of control most of the time, and that's not a good thing."

The strength in his hand when he grabbed hers surprised her. He gave a tug, drawing her toward him. "Promise me you won't leave. I need my own personal nurse when I get home. I want you there."

He was the most bullheaded man she'd ever met. "I will if you stop worrying about it and focus on getting better."

"Say. It."

She huffed. "I promise I will move in with you and never leave."

He smiled and closed his eyes, falling back to sleep.

She and the family took turns staying with him. A few hours later, he seemed more cognitive, if not just as annoying. He insisted on her raising the bed and letting him sit up, even though he was bandaged from his breastbone to his waist and needed to stay as flat as possible.

He screwed up his face as she raised him a couple inches, and she gave him a knowing glance. "See? You're gonna be sore for a long time. We have to restrict your activities."

"Bring me up to speed," he demanded. "We got Dover, right?"

"She's behind bars after being treated for a gunshot wound that I inflicted."

He gave her a thumbs up.

"Fortunately or unfortunately, Ali is dead."

"You again?"

Josie shook her head. "I injured her, but no. When Ronni tried to arrest her, she resisted. She had a gun hidden in her boot and attempted to take out a few agents. Things didn't go well for her."

Caleb looked serious, but not terribly upset. "That should put a crimp in her cartel."

"Bobby called and informed Malachi they're dismantling that as we speak. A dozen of her people have already been caught and charged."

"Now tell me we flushed out Glen, too."

"Nothing new there. Dover went to extreme lengths it appears to cover her tracks to him and made sure they couldn't be linked. Cooper sent two of his team to talk to Glen and Glen claims he never had any interaction with her."

"Any idea what he might've had that Dover still wanted so badly?"

"Nothing yet." She smoothed a hand over his blanket. "Maybe it was just a broken heart that came between them."

Caleb was silent, closing his eyes, and Josie wondered if he were already taxed from the conversation. She stayed quiet, watching him, happy that he at least had some color returning to his face.

She relaxed into the chair, prepared to wait until he woke up again, when he said, "I'll get you justice. You can count on it."

Her gaze snapped to his, his eyes clear and showing her the fighter inside.

That's all she needed right now. "I will handle it. Trust me I have a plan."

Caleb stared at her for several long seconds. "I love you," he said. "Especially how stubborn you are."

For the first time in a while she cracked a smile. "Ditto, rosebud."

TWENTY-NINE

T*wo weeks later*
Bondsman Brothers Agency

JOSIE FILED the latest closed case and waved at Ronni and Sam, coming to pick her up for lunch.

Caleb was recovering nicely and had returned to the office, although she was furious with him for going on an apprehension run. She was glad her new friends were going to distract her for the next hour over tacos and margaritas. "How's Thomas?"

"Back at work already." Ronni rested a hip against the desk. "Caleb?"

"Same." Josie put the phone on voicemail and grabbed her purse. "He's still sore, but he's out chasing a fugitive as we speak."

Sam laughed. "The Cahill brothers are nothing if not determined. I'm surprised he waited this long."

"Honestly, he seems as healthy as ever."

Apparently, something in her voice gave away the intimate detail of why she thought that. Ronni winked and gave her an elbow. "Nothing better than that kind of medicine to get you on your feet again."

Josie blushed, remembering their nightly activities. The good thing was, she was getting physical therapy again herself, and it was helping her hip immensely.

The bell over the door jingled as Caleb entered. He was sprouting a bruise on his cheek and had blood on two of his knuckles.

"Oh god," Josie said, exasperated. "Did you seriously get in a fight?"

Caleb didn't say a word as he moved aside to let two men file in. "This is Lee, the movie director, and Charles, head of the studio Glen sold your script to." He motioned at them. "Gentlemen, this is Josie Jackson."

Josie's mouth fell open, Sam and Ronni moving to each side of her.

Charles took a half step forward, almost as if he were going to offer a hand, and then simply gave her a nod. "We wanted to tell you in person that Glen Pember has been fired, his contract cancelled, and we're putting your name on everything."

She frowned at Caleb. "You threatened them, didn't you?"

Lee, shifting from one foot to the other, glanced out the window, as though wishing he were anywhere but here. "Mr. Pember is in Mr. Cahill's truck. It's come to our attention that he had an intimate relationship with a known fugitive, the Hollywood Hacker, and together they were blackmailing celebrities and politicians."

In between his words, Josie realized they were trying to distance themselves from what was sure to be a scandal that could rock the movie studio and all of those associated with it.

Thanks to Ronni, Josie had hired an attorney and knew she had a case against Glen.

Lee fished in a pocket and handed her a business card. "We encourage you to bring charges against Mr. Pember, as we will be doing, and would truly like to make things right with you. Your script, and the true-life story behind it, is worthy of the big screen. If you would like to negotiate with us, we're open to whatever deal you propose."

In other words, CYA. They needed to cover their assess.

She couldn't blame them, they probably had no idea Glen was dirty, but it still rankled.

She didn't accept the card, but Caleb did, tucking it in his back pocket. "I'm filing charges against the bastard as well." He pointed at his cheek. "He took a swing at me."

Charles and Lee said their goodbyes, again extending apologies and requesting further communication with Josie and reassuring her that she would have complete say in anything going forward if she chose to work with them.

After they exited, Josie rounded on Caleb. "You did it anyway. Even after I told you I'd handle it, you went after him."

He gingerly touched his injury. "You can beat me up later." He examined his bloody knuckles. "At the moment, I suggest you accept my grand gesture and get your attorney down here to negotiate the terms of your movie deal."

Sam patted her on the shoulder. "You should at least listen to their offer," she said.

Ronni nodded in agreement. "You can always shop it around to other studios, if you have a bad taste about this one. But I agree, at least hear them out. You're holding all the cards now, Josie."

At the look Caleb sent her, she realized she was holding more than just the cards to the movie. She was holding the relationship between them as well.

Stepping up to him, she lifted her chin. "You betrayed me again, by going behind my back and doing the exact thing I asked you not to."

He shot her a cheeky grin and playfully patted her cheek. "So sue me, buttercup. I love you, and that comes with a full-membership to the I-will-protect-you-at-all-costs package."

She punched his bicep, and then believing her luck had truly changed, she kissed him for everything she was worth.

When they broke apart, he grinned down at her. "Oorah."

She grinned back. "I love you, too."

Fatal Vision

Fatal Thrill

Risk

* * *

SEALS of Shadow Force Series: Spy Division

Man Hunt

Man Killer

Man Down

* * *

The Super Agent Series

Operation Sheba

Operation Paris

Operation Proof of Life

Operation Lost Princess

Operation Ambush

Operation Sleeping With the Enemy

* * *

The Justice Team Series (with Adrienne Giordano)

Stealing Justice

Cheating Justice

Holiday Justice

Exposing Justice

Undercover Justice

Protecting Justice

Missing Justice

Defending Justice

* * *

SCHOCK SISTERS MYSTERY SERIES w/Adrienne Giordano

1st Shock

2nd Strike

3rd Tango

* * *

The Secret Ingredient Culinary Mystery Series

The Secret Ingredient, A Culinary Romantic Mystery with Bonus Recipes

The Secret Life of Cranberry Sauce, A Secret Ingredient Holiday Novella

Paranormal Romance

Witches Anonymous Step 1

Jingle Hells, Witches Anonymous Step 2

Wicked Souls, Witches Anonymous Step 3

Dark Moon Lilith, Witches Anonymous Step 4

Dancing With the Devil, Witches Anonymous Step 5

Devil's Due, Witches Anonymous Step 6

Dirty Deeds, Witches Anonymous Step 7

Wicked Wedding, Witches Anonymous Step 8

Urban Fantasy

Revenge Is Sweet, Kali Sweet Urban Fantasy Series, Book 1

Sweet Chaos, Kali Sweet Urban Fantasy Series, Book 2

Sweet Soldier, Kali Sweet Urban Fantasy Series, Book 3

Sweet Curse, Kali Sweet Urban Fantasy Series, Book 4

Paranormal Romantic Suspense

Soul Survivor, Moon Water Series, Book 1

Soul Protector, Moon Water Series, Book 2

* * *

Cozy Mysteries (writing as Nyx Halliwell)

Sister Witches Of Raven Falls Mystery Series

Of Potions and Portents

Of Curses and Charms

Of Stars and Spells

Of Spirits and Superstition

Confessions of a Closet Medium Cozy Mystery Series

Pumpkins & Poltergeists

Magic & Mistletoe

Haunts & Hearts (Spring 2021)

Once Upon a Witch Cozy Mystery Series

If the Cursed Shoe Fits (Cinder)

Beastly Book of Spells (Belle) August 2020

Poisoned Apple Potion (Snow) October 2020

Red Hot Wolfie (Ruby) January 2021

Hexed Hair Day (Rapunzel) April 2021

MEET MISTY

USA TODAY Bestselling Author Misty Evans has published more than sixty novels and writes romantic suspense, urban fantasy, and paranormal romance. Under her pen name, Nyx Halliwell, she also writes cozy mysteries.

She got her start writing in 4th grade when she won second place in a school writing contest with an essay about her dad. Since then, she's written nonfiction magazine articles, started her own coaching business, become a yoga teacher, and raised twin boys on top of enjoying her fiction career.

When not reading or writing, she enjoys music, movies, and hanging out with her husband, twin sons, and three spoiled puppies. A registered yoga teacher and Master Reiki Practitioner, she shares her love of chakra yoga and energy healing, but still hasn't mastered levitating.

Get free reads, all the latest news, and alerts about sales when you sign up for her newsletter at www.readmistyevans.com. Check out her humorous pen name Nyx Halliwell for magical mysteries https://www.nyxhalliwell.com.

LETTER FROM MISTY

Hello Beautiful Reader!

Thank you for reading this story! It is an honor and a privilege to write stories for you.

I hope you enjoyed this book, and I'd like to ask a favor – would you mind leaving a review at your favorite retailer? I'd really appreciate it, and reviews help other readers find books they will love too.

If you'd like to learn about my other books, sales, and special promotions, please sign up for my newsletter at www.readmistyevans.com.

Grab special edition box sets and get new releases before they come out at retailers by visiting my direct buy website www.mistyevansbooks.com. I have sales and offer NEW RELEASES early and at a discount!! Check it out.

I also have a holistic business, Crystals With Misty, and invite you to check out my website www.crystalswithmisty.com for information on my services.

Last but not least, if you enjoy clean, cozy mysteries, visit my pen name www.nyxhalliwell.com to see those books!

Thank you and happy reading!

Misty